PANIC POINT

BOOK TWO – THE PEPPERMAN MYSTERY SERIES

PANIC POINT

BOOK TWO – THE PEPPERMAN MYSTERY SERIES

BILL BRISCOE

Editor: Lori Freeland
Cover Designer: Fiona Jayde Media
Formatting: The Deliberate Page

Available in eBook & Paperback

eBook ISBN: 978-0-9986425-5-0
Paperback ISBN: 978-0-9986425-6-7

http://billbriscoe.com

This book is dedicated to the memory of Larry Hauser,
a friend and mentor.
Boomer!

CHAPTER 1

August 1993
Great Smoky Mountain National Park

A LARGE GUST OF WIND BLASTED THE TENT, THEN AS SUDDENLY as it came, it was over. I turned on my left side and watched Morgan sleep. My new bride lay cuddled in her sleeping bag in our small two-person tent, each of her slow, easy breaths bringing me peace.

Special Ops missions sucked the life right out of you. You couldn't know true evil until you saw evidence of people burned alive, children beheaded for playing soccer, or women taken from their homes and never seen again.

But I wasn't going to let those events dominate my life. No, I had Morgan. And she was just the softness my rough Navy SEAL edges needed. The third day of our honeymoon and marriage was proof of that.

"Good morning," she said in a slow, soft voice without opening her steel-blue eyes. I swear those eyes combined with that creamy mocha skin, so many shades lighter than mine, could bring Big Foot to his knees.

I reached over and stroked her sculptured cheekbone and jawline, her face a combination of strength and beauty.

The corners of her lips peaked upward. The tips of her fingers and her long muscular legs reached from one end of the tent to the other.

I leaned forward and kissed her forehead. "Good morning."

"What are you getting ready to do?" She sat up, wrapping her arms around her pulled-up knees.

I unzipped my sleeping bag and slipped on my cargo pants. Pulling a camo T-shirt over my head, I looked around the tent. "Where are my socks and combat boots?"

Her impish giggle had an edge of orneriness. "I told you last night not to leave them outside."

I picked up my pillow and tossed it her way. "A good wife would've brought them inside."

"A thoughtful husband would've thanked me for the reminder."

"Okay. Should've listened." Although I hadn't been married long, it was long enough to know I needed to wiggle myself out of this tight spot.

"Of course." She gave me a wink and an easy nod. "What are you going to do right now?"

I pulled back the flap of the tent and saw my boots and dirty socks where I left them. "I'm going down to the waterfalls about a half mile from camp. You want to come?"

"No, I'll start breakfast. How long will you be?"

"Thirty minutes. Will that be long enough for you to make yourself beautiful for your fantastic husband?"

"Careful big boy." She lowered her chin and looked up at me with a stare that said, *don't go there*. Then a Colgate smile spread across her cheeks.

I gave her a proper military salute. "Yes, ma'am."

"Oh, Earl, before you go, would you loosen the rope and lower our food from the tree cable? I'll get the salt pork frying and cook some powdered eggs."

The tent didn't allow me to stand so I knelt on both knees, put my hands on her cheeks, and gave her a good kiss. "You're the best, and you look great when you first wake up."

She gave me a gentle nudge. "Flattery will go a long way."

I pushed through the tent flap and stood. The August day was foggy with a bit of chill in the air. The beauty of the Great Smoky Mountains of Tennessee was spellbinding. Crows squawked in the distance. A gentle breeze pushed its way through the tops of yellow birch trees, slowly moving the branches. A squirrel scampered across our campsite, paused and munched on his breakfast, oblivious to me.

I turned toward the tent. "Morgan, do you want me to leave the pistol? There might be wild boars in this area."

She stuck her head out, her hair a mess.

Cute. My heart rate ticked up a notch or two. I knew we belonged together.

"Nope," she said. "Won't need it."

I put my old service handgun, a durable Sig Sauer P226, in my holster and headed toward the falls. The mountain was steep and the forest dense with undergrowth. I had to angle and twist my way through straight, large birch trees. Morgan's choice for the honeymoon was the perfect spot for me to unwind.

When I reached the spectacular falls, its power was overwhelming. The awesome roar of the churning water made me feel insignificant. I balanced against a rock, cupped my hand, filled it with the pure, clean, cold water, and splashed it on my face. It took my breath.

I was mesmerized for fifteen or twenty minutes sitting next to the stream. Then a weird feeling that someone was watching spiked my adrenalin. Hand on my gun, I looked around, but saw no one. Heard no one.

But still, an icy chill plucked up every hair on the back of my neck. The high-pitched scream of a cougar spread panic through my body like a kindling fire. Morgan. I had to get back to Morgan.

As I pulled my pistol, it started to rain. I raced up the mountain, weaving in and out of the trees, my lungs pounding. When I reached camp, I stopped so fast I fell onto the muddy ground.

The tent was crumpled. Salt pork smoldered in the pan. Powdered eggs were scattered next to the fire.

My legs felt like they'd been beaten with a rubber mallet. Paralysis set in, my feet anchored in cement. "Morgan!" I lowered the gun to my side and screamed for my wife over and over.

But she was gone.

CHAPTER 2

Six Months Earlier
Belleville, New Jersey

I WOKE UP IN MY DUPLEX AT 6:45 A.M., MY TOOTH THROBBING like someone had taken a jackhammer to it. The throbbing and the *tick, tick, tick* of the clock were in perfect sync. I thumbed through a sports magazine until the alarm went off at 7:30. Didn't remember a thing I read. How could I concentrate?

I was twenty-eight, but the first person I wanted to see wasn't a doctor. Mamma should be at the diner. I showered, dressed, and headed to the restaurant, parking in the back.

My thoughts drifted to the diner and the day Mr. Leitner sold it to Mamma for five dollars. His way of paying her back for all the years she'd worked there. She'd turned it into the best BBQ place in New Jersey. People loved her baby back ribs so much their taste buds and tongues did the stadium wave.

I don't know how she raised Burl, Tony, Belinda, Mary Nelle, and me by herself. Dad's death when Burl and I were babies put a serious strain on the family.

"Come on in. You hungry?" She must've seen me drive up because she anchored the door with her beef-cake hip and let me slide by.

"My tooth hurts." I rubbed my jaw. "I need to see Dr. Brady. When does his office open? Am I still on your dental policy?"

She tapped me on the backside as I walked by. "Which question you want me to answer first?" I loved her guttural laugh. It made me feel warm like cinnamon toast on a snowy morning. "I'll call and see if they're open."

She slipped on her round, red reading glasses. They looked like diving goggles. She pulled the phone book from the drawer, flipped through the pages, and dialed the number. "This is Glynna Helmsly. Is Dr. Brady in? Hmmm...my son Earl's tooth is bothering him. Is there someone else he can see? He's hurting somethin' terrible....Okay, I'll send him right down."

After hanging up and removing those gosh-awful glasses, Mamma scratched her head. "Dr. Brady's not in today, but Dr. Whitten will see you at nine o'clock."

I didn't remember a Dr. Whitten at the dental office. But I was desperate. Big brother Tony wouldn't be expecting me at my job at his grappling club in Newark until after lunch. That would give the dentist plenty of time to ruin my day before I went to work.

Mamma pointed with a pink-painted fingernail to the chair in front of her desk. "Sit down. Open up. Let me see in there." She unzipped a purse that could double for an overnight bag, pulled out her car keys, and walked around the desk.

"You're not going to pry my tooth out, are you?" I said it half-joking and half-serious. Mamma had pulled my baby teeth with a pair of pliers.

"Open up, sugar foot." She flicked on a small flashlight fastened to her key chain, stooped to shine the light into my mouth, then pulled back—her eyes the size of matzo balls.

"Lord, have mercy, Earl. You've got a cavity big enough to hide a shoe. When was the last time you went to the dentist?"

"Don't know. I was still in the Navy."

"Get on down to Dr. Brady's, you hear."

"Okay." I pushed out of the chair, reached over, and gave her a hug. "Just don't try to pull my tooth with those rusty pliers you had when I was a kid."

She gave me a near kiss on my cheek. "Go on…and you ain't on no dental policy."

I pulled into Doc Brady's parking lot at 9:05, a bit uneasy. He was the only dentist at this clinic to work on me, and the only one I trusted. I walked up to the door. Etched in the glass was what looked like a tooth with two eyes and a mouth. Clever advertising. The waiting room was empty. Everybody in Belleville had probably heard Dr. Brady was not in and cancelled their appointments. Dr. Whitten was probably sixteen with zero experience. Just my luck.

The receptionist looked up. Her beautiful straight, white teeth made her the poster girl for Dr. Brady's handiwork.

"I'm Earl Helmsly, here to see Dr. Whitten."

"Yes, Mr. Helmsly. Dr. Whitten will be with you shortly." She took me down a long hallway to the last room on the right. The walls were plastered with pictures of little kids.

I adjusted my 6' 2", two hundred thirty-pound body the best I could on the long, slender reclining chair.

On the wall directly in front of me was a framed diploma with Dr. Whitten's name on it. A graduate of the University of Tennessee Dental School. Oh, good grief, not only a rookie dentist, but a southerner. Wouldn't be able to understand a word he said. He'd probably sound like Colonel Sanders with a couple of marbles in his mouth.

I lay back in the chair waiting for my torture session. The ceiling was covered with peaceful landscapes and photos of cats and dogs. What was that all about? Lack of sleep caught up with me. I dozed off.

"Mr. Helmsly. Mr. Helmsly."

I rubbed my eyes with my thumb and index finger, trying to focus. Standing before me was a beautiful woman with almond-shaped blue eyes. Her athletic body was tall and lean. I'd seen pictures of Miss America Vanessa Williams. This had to be her sister.

"I'm Dr. Whitten."

I rubbed my eyes again. "Say what?"

"I'm Dr. Whitten." The tone of her voice gave away that she might be irritated by my question.

I looked at the diploma, then back at Miss Too Good To Be True. "Dr. Morgan Whitten?"

She angled her head and gave me a smug smile. I think she was making fun of me. "Yes," she drew the word out.

Yup, she was making fun. "But you're not a guy."

"If I am, I've got a lot of explaining to do."

My gaze went to her hand. No wedding ring. This might not be such a bad day after all.

CHAPTER 3

Six months ago, I'd sat in a dental chair and asked Morgan to go out with me. Now we were getting married in a few days. Amused at how situations could change in a heartbeat, I took a sip of Diet Dr. Pepper and choked. The soda fire-hosed through the gaps in my teeth and all over the steering wheel. Bummer. Where was a napkin when I needed one? Using my forearm, I swiped the sticky wheel. What good did that do?

I pulled in front of Jim Pepperman's mom's house in Belleville, New Jersey. The morning was cool, birds chirped, and the manicured grass added to the pristine setting. Tomorrow, we'd head out on the nine-hour trip to Elizabethton, Tennessee, my fiancé's hometown.

Jim offered to make the drive with me. He'd flown in two days earlier from Bartlesville, Oklahoma. My twin, Burl, had put him in charge of organizing my bachelor party. The Newark Grappling Club, owned by Tony and managed by Burl, had a wrestling tournament scheduled mid-week with its biggest rival — the Inner City Club in Brooklyn. They couldn't leave when I did.

"Come on in." Jim met me at the door. "Mom's anxious to see you." His massive shoulders and small waist made him look like he could still play for the

Pittsburgh Steelers. Our skin color didn't match and we had different last names, but he was still my brother. My family would walk the plank for his family and vice versa.

The aroma of homemade bread brought back childhood memories of cold Saturday mornings. The smell pulled me through the living room into the kitchen like a magnet. I wanted a plate full of Mrs. Pepperman's golden brown rolls.

She opened the oven door and slipped the tray of heaven's delight onto the counter.

I reached one arm around her and angled the other toward the bread pan.

"They're too hot." She tapped my knuckles. "You'll burn your fingers."

I gave her a kiss on the forehead and wrapped both arms around her small, round shoulders. "Okay, but you know I can't resist too long. Gotta have my rolls, butter, honey, and a big glass of milk."

She tugged on my cheek with her thumb and index finger. "You little rascal, you haven't changed a bit. Let me get a plate."

I glanced at Jim leaning against the door frame. His eyes seemed to sparkle as he slowly patted his heart.

"Where did you learn to make dinner rolls?" I briskly rubbed my hands together anticipating the first bite.

She looked over the finished product as she touched my shoulder, then placed the plate in front of me. "Jim's grandmother passed the recipe down, but I never quite mastered her cooking techniques when it came to bread making."

I pulled the chair away from the wooden Amish table and sat. "I can't believe her rolls were any better than yours."

There was a lightness in her smile when she looked at me. Love didn't always have to be spoken.

I slapped creamy butter on both halves of the bread, doused a large tablespoon of honey in the middle, and dug in, gorging myself like I'd never eat again.

Jim pulled a chair next to me and managed to steal a few round mounds of bread. "Can't let you have all the enjoyment. Pass that butter and honey."

Jim's mother backed against the kitchen sink, folding her hands inside a white kitchen towel. The soft expression on her face indicated she was thoroughly enjoying watching us eat.

I licked the honey from my fingers. "How's Laura?"

"She's excited about the wedding," Jim said. "She and our boys are flying in on Friday."

We visited nearly an hour and a half and finished off the plate of bread. "I'll pick you up a little before six in the morning." I looked forward to the trip with Jim. Lots to catch up on.

The sun broke over the horizon when I pulled up to get him. The light in the living room was visible from the street. I jogged to the front of the house and barged in. No need to knock.

The living room smelled like fresh cinnamon rolls. My nostrils flared and drew in as much sweet pleasure as possible. I needed to get out of Belleville before I gained twenty pounds.

Didn't have to wait on Jim. He met me in the kitchen just as his mom placed the rolls in a paper sack. She turned us toward the car, placed her hands on our shoulders, and pushed, telling us to hit the road.

We pulled out of Belleville at 6:00 a.m. making a quick stop at Dunkin' Donuts for coffee. As we pulled onto Highway 87 toward Baltimore, Jim started laughing.

"What's going on?"

He scratched his chin and broke out in a grin before giving me a playful slap on my arm with the back of his left hand.

I glanced over. "What?"

"Remember the first time I met you and your family? The moment I stepped onto the sidewalk leading up to your house, you and Burl raced up to me. You grabbed one leg, Burl the other. I had to walk like Frankenstein to the steps, dragging you two bags of cement."

"Really." I didn't remember that. "How old were we?"

"About three. I knew then you guys were special, and I was right."

"I do remember when Burl and I were in grade school, you and Tony ran us out of the house because we were being pests."

"I never said you were angels." Jim laughed. "There were times Tony and I wanted to run an ad in the Belleville newspaper offering to sell the both of you for two bits and a firm handshake. But God blessed my family when He brought yours into our lives." He grabbed the back of my neck. "Now tell me how in the blazes did you meet a Tennessee girl?"

The thought of Morgan swelled my chest like white caps on the ocean. I tapped my thumbs on the steering wheel. "Do you remember Doc Brady?"

"Sure, everyone in Belleville knows the tooth doctor."

"Well, his daughter Kaura went to dental school at the University of Tennessee. Morgan was there at the same time, and they became friends. Six months ago I had the mother of all toothaches. Dr. Brady was out that day, but the receptionist worked me into Morgan's schedule."

"Ah, love at first sight, right?"

"You got it. Things fast-forwarded and here we are."

"So, you really need to be thankful Doc Brady offered Morgan a job."

"Yes, sir. You bet your boots."

Our conversations centered around our families the rest of the trip. It was late afternoon when we pulled into Elizabethton—population 11,931.

"Jim, look." Just ahead on the right was a billboard that read Morgan Whitten, 1984 State Champion, Girls 200 Meters. Under Morgan's name was Jordan Zeka, 1985 State Champion, Girls Discus. "Morgan told me she ran track at the University of Tennessee, but she never mentioned she was a state champion in high school."

Jim leaned back as far as he could and stretched. "Well, we know Elizabethton has raised some great women athletes. Wonder if they'll ever have a male superstar coming out of this town?"

"Hard to say, but a small town like this probably will have only great high school athletes. The odds are against a Hall of Fame guy coming from Elizabethton. Won't happen."

CHAPTER 4

When Jim and I pulled in front of Morgan's mother's house, Morgan stepped out wearing an orange Tennessee Vols T-shirt and tight jeans. *Zowie.*

She stretched her hand high on the porch column, bent one knee, and did her best Marilyn Monroe pose. "Who's that homely guy walking up my sidewalk?"

I loved her sexy southern drawl. I wagged my finger at her, then stretched out my arms. "A special, loving greeting from my fiancée." My words were laced with playful sarcasm, and I ran up the steps, pulled her warm body to mine, and planted a kiss on her perfectly-shaped lips. *Fire.*

Morgan wrapped her arms around me. "You bring out the hopelessly-in-love woman in me." She loosened her grip and leaned back, almost bouncing on her toes. "The house has become wedding central. Our gifts outnumber the hairs on my head."

"If that's the case, your mom must have built another room."

"You're so funny…looking."

I liked it when she jabbed me. Before I could kiss her again, Jim "Ahem'd" me from behind. I stepped back. "Morgan, meet Jim Pepperman, my brother from another mother."

"Welcome, Mr. Pepperman." She extended her right hand and gave him a healthy handshake.

Jim leaned in. "You're family. We don't shake hands, we hug."

Morgan's eyes said everything that needed to be said. She liked him.

We walked into the house just as Morgan's mom came in through the back door, her red and white do-rag cocked to one side.

"Momma, this is Mr. Pepperman."

Jim waved his hand and shook his head. "Please, call me Jim."

Morgan pushed her hair to the side and nodded. "Okay, Jim. This is Melody, my mom."

Melody side-stepped the clean laundry basket, placed both hands on Jim's shoulders, and gave a gentle push as though she was checking his stability. "You're a big rascal."

"Momma, I want to show Jim what Earl got me for a wedding present." Morgan speed-walked us across the living room into the den. "Look, a tent."

Jim soured his lips and pointed. "He got you a tent?"

"A two-person tent. For our honeymoon."

Jim shook his head and smiled like a junkyard dog with a mess of chitlins. "A tent?"

Morgan interlocked her arm through mine and grinned. "Camping is my passion, been doing it for years. Told Earl I'd marry him if he'd take me to the Smoky Mountains for our honeymoon."

"You are one unique young lady." Jim placed his hand on Morgan's shoulder and gave it a gentle rock. "You're going to fit in with this family."

"Alone on top of a mountain with Earl." She kissed my cheek. "What could possibly be better?"

"Enough about honeymoons," Morgan's mom interrupted. "You like fried okra, Jim?"

"Yes, ma'am, a favorite of mine."

"You're gonna get a mess of it tonight. Earl, let's go pick 'em."

Melody's generous hips bounced from side to side as I followed her through the kitchen and out the back door.

CHAPTER 5

I FOLLOWED MELODY THROUGH THE KITCHEN.

She grabbed two brown paper bags as we walked out the rickety, red screen door to her garden. Without stopping, she reached back and passed me a sack. "You be a city folk. Don't pick the real long okra. Too tough to eat. Just get the ones about three inches." She pointed to the straight, manicured rows. "You go down that one. I'll go down this one." She reached inside her apron pocket, pulled out one of those little black cigars that looked like a cigarette, lit it, inhaled, blew out a cloud of smoke that reminded me of a pufferbelly locomotive, then started out.

I let her stay about a yard ahead of me and watched her select the right size okra, then copied her pick.

She sang Aretha Franklin's "I'll Say a Little Prayer" as she went down the row, her voice mellow, and her soprano tone right on pitch.

I wondered if that song was aimed my direction.

A little while later, she waved to a large pecan tree at the end of the garden. "Let's go sit a spell and talk. We got enough okra for tonight." She pulled up an old, wooden rocker that groaned when she sat and placed the sack beside her. Then she pinched her cigar stub between her thumb and middle finger and flipped it a good ten feet, dead center into a trash can. Michael Jordan couldn't have done any better with a basketball. She pointed to a rusty, green metal lawn chair across from her.

I sat, wiping sweat from my brow with the side of my index finger. "I'm impressed with your flipping skills. How'd you do that?"

"Don't know. Just comes natural." Melody smiled as though she had a story to tell. "One day when Morgan was eight, I'd walked down to Redi Mart to get some bread. When I got home, she sat on the porch, puffing on one of my cigarillos. I put the bread down and asked if I could join her. She slid the smoke to the corner of her mouth, handed me the pack, and said, 'Help yourself.' Oh, she thought she was the Queen of Sheba. We sat and talked for awhile. She began to rub her stomach, then lay back on the porch clamping a hand over her mouth. She got sick as an old dog that ate too many hush puppies. Never smoked again."

She pulled her yellow skirt to her knees, then steepled her fingers. Her big eyes narrowed to tiny coin slots. She stared at me like I'd stolen a blue-ribbon watermelon. "You gonna treat my baby girl right, Earl?"

I paused before answering. Where was she going with that question? "Yes, ma'am."

"You were a Navy SEAL, right?"

"Yes, ma'am."

"In the animal kingdom, a seal has no chance against a momma walrus. You wanna guess what kind of momma I am?"

Oh, shoot. How would I answer that? "You'd be a walrus."

Her narrowed eyes widened as large as a Moon Pie. "You calling me a walrus?"

"Yes, ma'am. I mean nooo ma'am." I made a crossing motion with my hands. "I'm not calling you a walrus."

Melody leaned back in her chair, threw her head back, slapped both knees, and laughed the kind of laugh that would make a grumpy old man smile. "You didn't catch my drift, son. I was making a comparison of a momma walrus protecting her baby. Just like I'm protecting my baby."

"I'd never mistreat Morgan. I have too much love and respect for her. She's my best friend."

There was a long pause as though she was thinking about our conversation, then she busted out hee-hawing again, got up, and rubbed my head. "You alright, son. Morgan picked her a good 'en. Let's go get this okra ready for cookin'."

That one moment brought me closer to Morgan's mom. She reminded me of my mamma—strong and independent.

CHAPTER 6

I GRABBED MORGAN BY THE HAND, AND WE RACED TO THE car under a shower of rice that felt like pellets of sleet.

"Earl, hurry…open the door." Morgan bounced up and down, giggling, trying to evade the overexuberant wedding guests.

I fumbled with the keys. "I'm trying. Are you kidding me? Someone taped the keys together." My smile freeze-framed. My little idiot sisters had to be the ones who pulled the prank. "Belinda and Mary Nelle borrowed the keys to put a special gift in the backseat." I managed to tear away the Scotch tape, open the door, and push Morgan across the front seat.

"I will never forget August 14, 1993, the day I became Mrs. Earl Helmsly." Her hands, pressed over her lips, muffled laughter, or was it tears?

Jamming the key into the ignition, I pulled out of the church parking lot and headed toward Gatlinburg. We drove several miles without saying a word. I suppose both of us were trying to put things in perspective. One tear eased down Morgan's face. I reached over and touched her knee. "Are you okay?"

She placed her hand on my cheek. "Better than okay. You've made my life complete. I never imagined I could love someone so much."

I didn't know what to say but had to say something. "Burl and I had an albino frog we kept in a fish tank by our bed. I loved that frog, just like I love you."

Morgan slapped the back of my head. "You're such a romantic."

"What can I say?" I hunched my shoulders. "That frog was special."

"You never had a frog. Your mom would've told me." Morgan tickled my ribcage, causing me to swerve the car.

"Okay, I never had a frog. Stop digging your fingers under my ribs."

She gave me another love tap, this time to my bicep.

Finding one's soul mate was a blessing. That could never be truer than for Morgan and me. I'd never had a toothache before that day, and her being the only dentist available was my good fortune. Divine intervention? You'd never convince me otherwise.

We pulled into Greeneville, Tennessee, about 10:00 o'clock to spend the night. A big sign stretched across Main Street, *Greene County Fair*.

Morgan leaned forward placing one hand on the dash. "Did you make us a reservation?"

I shook my head. "Nope. Didn't think I needed to. Small towns always have vacancies."

"Uh huh." Morgan nodded. "Unless it's during the Greene County Fair." Every word was articulated precisely.

We drove by all the motels in town. The *no vacancy* signs couldn't have been bigger or brighter. I finally pulled into the Quality Inn. "Surely someone had to cancel at the last moment." I got back in the car sixty seconds later. "No go."

The dome light haloed Morgan's face. Her eyes narrowed, and she raised both hands in a strangling motion. Didn't have to be a mind reader to guess what she was thinking.

We headed west about twenty-five miles to the booming town of Newport. The only motel we came to was the Eckland. It looked like it was constructed in the early 1940s with zero updates. We were fortunate...or not. Ye Old Eckland had fourteen rooms and fourteen vacancies. I chose room number seven. Maybe that would change our luck.

"I'm going to carry you over the threshold just like they do in the movies." I put the old-fashioned key in the slot and turned the door handle. Nothing happened. Tried again. Same results. I slammed my shoulder into the paint-chipped red door. It gave way, hurling me inside, landing a perfect belly flop on the rose-patterned rug.

Morgan laughed so hard she slapped the door frame with her open hand and doubled over. "Why don't I just walk in and save you the trouble?"

I rolled over and sat up, wrapping my arms around my knees. "Good idea. Let's not make this complicated."

The picture on the wall was of Franklin Delano Roosevelt. I peeked behind the frame. It looked like the photo hadn't been moved since the day it was hung. The once-white lamp shades were now cream- colored with light bulb burns on the sides. It was impossible to tell whether the bedspread was originally red or pink.

Morgan was a good sport, and we made it just fine. I suppose things could have been worse, but I didn't know how.

CHAPTER 7

THE FIRST NIGHT OF OUR HONEYMOON AT THE ECKLAND MOTEL was a night to remember. The old, broken-down building would be something we'd talk about forever. If I had the power to do it over, I wouldn't change a thing. Morgan's good-natured smile during the whole mess indicated she wouldn't change it either.

We slept in that morning. The Bloodhound Café served me a good breakfast of pancakes, eggs, bacon, wheat toast, and orange juice. Morgan went a lighter route of oatmeal, toast, and fruit that would've lasted me fifteen minutes. I gave her a hard time about her picky diet.

After breakfast, we pulled onto Highway 321 West headed to Gatlinburg. Morgan loved maps. She opened the State Farm road atlas and picked out every sightseeing spot along the way.

Growing up, she didn't have a father or brother, and I wondered how she'd developed such an interest in the outdoors. "Hey, what started you backcountry camping?"

"My cousins live in Franklin County. I'd go there in the summertime, and we'd camp in the Cumberland Mountains."

"What town is that close to?"

She took off her reading glasses, rubbed the bridge of her nose, and slid them back on her face. "Winchester."

"Are we going to Winchester?"

Morgan looked at me like I was crazy. "Heck, no. Jerre and Johnny would want to come with us." She pointed straight ahead. "Keep your eyes on the road."

I grinned and gave her a thumbs-up. She had a way of making me happy. It wasn't what she said, but the way she said it with that small voice inflection at just the right time. And her smile made me glow inside. Morgan was the real deal.

Pulling into Pigeon Forge, Tennessee, seven miles from Gatlinburg, I noticed the Memories Live Entertainment Theater. "Look, Morgan. They're doing a tribute to Frankie Valli and the Four Seasons. Frankie was born in Belleville, New Jersey. I grew up listening to his songs. You want to see if we can get tickets for tonight?"

She shrugged. "Sure, but the sign says the show starts at 6:30 p.m., and it's 6:00 now."

The parking lot looked jammed, but what the heck, wouldn't hurt to try. We pulled to the far end of the lot, parked, and ran to the front.

The ticket taker's name tag read Kym. "How can I help you?"

"Got two tickets for tonight's show?"

"No, sir. Sold out." She flipped through her reservations list. "We do have tickets available tomorrow."

I rolled my lips and popped them. "Shoot, won't work. We're going backcountry camping." I leaned forward, placing my hands on the counter. "Kym, this is our honeymoon. We were married yesterday." I spoke with a soft, persuasive tone. "I really want my wife to hear these songs. It's special to me. Frankie Valli and I are from the same hometown. Is there any way you can let us in? I'll pay double if I have to. It's that important."

Kym picked up a pen and tapped her lips. "I'm not supposed to do this. The seating capacity is full, but I can give you two folding chairs for the back wall. Will that work?"

I extended my arms to the ceiling. "Yes. Thank you," I whispered.

"That'll be thirty dollars." Her smile was warm and genuine.

I paid her, took Morgan's hand, and walked toward the theater door.

"Sir, what's your name?" Kym called after us.

I turned. "Earl, and this is my wife Morgan."

"See the girl at the concession stand for the folding chairs. Her name is Bell. She's my daughter. Tell her I said you could use them and to give you two soft drinks and two popcorns on the house."

I acted as though I was tipping my hat. Southern hospitality was everything it was pumped up to be. The show was sensational, but that's not what I'd remember. Kym's kindness went above and beyond for two honeymooners. I'd think of this night every time I heard a Four Season's song.

The full moon highlighted the trees when we left the theater. I could almost feel a part of nature's magnificence. At that moment, man and mountain were united in one glorious spirit.

CHAPTER 8

After the Four Seasons show in Pigeon Forge, Morgan and I made the short drive to Gatlinburg and spent the night at The Mountain Inn. Sleep came easy. The bed was a hundred times better than at the Eckland.

The obnoxiously loud radio clock went off at 7:00 a.m.

"Get up, city boy." Morgan slapped my backside. "We've got a long day."

"What's the hurry? We're on honeymoon time." I yawned and stretched, wanting another hour of sleep.

Morgan headed toward the bathroom. "The honeymoon's over if you don't get on the move." She peeked out from behind the door, then giggled as she shut it.

My feet hit the floor.

At 7:45 a.m., we pulled into the crowded parking lot of Log Cabin Pancake House. I couldn't wait to see what Morgan would order. They'd laugh her out of the place if she wanted a bowl of fruit with non-fat yogurt.

The sign at the door entrance read *Seat Yourself.* We took a table by the big picture window. The sun was just breaking over the mountains. The flood of yellow light seemed to warm the sky. A small rain cloud pushed its way over the tree tops. One hawk made lazy circles in

the fresh air near the top of the mountain, no doubt looking for his breakfast.

A tall waitress approached our table. She was attractive,
but her skin looked pale and her eyes sunken as though
she hadn't slept. "What can I get you folks to drink?"

Morgan smiled. "I'll have water with a slice of lemon."

The waitress looked down at me. "What about you?"

"The same thing, but bring me a large glass of orange
juice too."

"You ready to order?" One hand on her hip,
she yawned.

Morgan placed the tip of her index finger on her right
temple making a scratching motion, probably looking
over the menu for that wuss breakfast of yogurt and
berries. "Earl, go ahead. I'm not quite ready."

Ah ha, I was right. She couldn't find that sissy stuff.

The waitress turned to me, pen ready. "I'll have two
eggs over medium, hash browns, bacon, and wheat toast."

I couldn't wait to hear what my bride wanted.

"I'll have the bowl of mixed fruit...with one pancake,
one over-medium egg, one slice of ham, a plate of hash
browns, and biscuits."

My chin not only hit the table but bounced up and
down three times.

"What?" Morgan shrugged "I'm hungry."

My life with this woman was going to be one surprise after another.

Both of us scarfed down our meals as though they
were our last.

I guessed the waitress noticed our empty plates. She
approached us with the ticket. "Have a wonderful day."

"Excuse me, ma'am. My wife and I are going back-country camping and need a few things. Could you direct us to the closest outdoor supply store?"

She stuck her order pad in the front pocket of her apron and the ink pen behind her ear. "Are you heading out from Newfound Gap?"

"Yes." I said.

"Maw Tuttle's Last Chance Store is on the right just as you leave town. She should have everything you need."

"Thanks for your help." I nodded. "Oh hey, one other thing. Thanks for the great service." I wanted to make her smile.

And she did. "You folks come again."

I finished off my orange juice and slipped a twenty dollar tip on the table.

Morgan used her palm to muffle a burp. Her eyes darted left, then right. Appearing a little embarrassed, she straightened in her chair, lifted her chin and pro-claimed, "Not bad manners, just good food."

If that wasn't, cliché nothing was. "I'm sure Emily Pool would overlook that etiquette mishap."

Morgan tapped her mouth with a napkin. Her nose turned upward so high if it rained she would drown. "If you're talking about the lady who wrote the book on table etiquette, her name is Emily Post, not Emily Pool." She dipped her head and started to laugh.

I loved the way Morgan got an innocent, almost child-like expression without even realizing she'd done it.

A light rain showered us as we walked to the car. The weather forecast for the next few days predicted no rain, maybe just a passing cloud. By the time we reached the camping store the rain stopped.

Couldn't miss Maw Tuttle's. The sign was as big as a Greyhound bus. The building had a long, covered wooden porch with two rockers on each side of the door. Brass spittoons reminded me of pictures I'd seen of country stores in the 1930s. Once inside, the throwback years didn't stop. An old cracker barrel sat next to the cash register. Glass jars of hard candy lined the shelves on the wall. The store was stocked with all sorts of camping equipment, rain gear, pup tents, thick, white hiking socks, and ball caps of all colors stacked neatly on top of each other.

"Hello." I look around but saw no one. "Anyone here? Hello."

What happened next completed the old-fashioned flashback. A little old lady stepped from behind a drawn curtain over the doorway in the back of the building looking like Granny from *The Beverly Hillbillies*. Her gray hair was pulled back in a bun, small wire-framed glasses perched on the end of a button nose, and black lace-up boots accentuated her pink-and-blue-flowered dress.

You had to be kidding me.

She walked toward us, pushing the glasses back on her face. "How can I help you?"

I looked down at the perky little woman. "I bet you'd be Maw Tuttle."

When she smiled, only one corner of her mouth moved. Maybe she'd had a small stroke. "You'd be right, sonny. What can I help you with?"

"We need freeze-dried food. That's about it."

Maw Tuttle pointed to the front of the building on the wall next to a clothing rack. "We have a good assortment. If you like beef stroganoff, you might wanna to give it a try. How are you going to heat it?"

"Campfire. Glad you reminded me. I need a utility lighter."

Maw jutted out her chin and shook her head. "Not a good idea to start a campfire — against the law. A park ranger catches you, a heavy fine will follow. What you need is a small, lightweight, two-burner stove. Runs on butane. Very safe."

"Morgan?" I turned to look at my wife. "Did you know we can't build a campfire?"

She rummaged through a stack of plaid shirts on sale. "Nope. We built fires in the Cumberland Mountains. Better get a stove, honey. Don't want to take a chance on getting a fine."

I shrugged.

"My new bride said 'Yes,' Maw." I gave Morgan a quick glance and saw her smile while she kept shuffling through the stack of shirts.

Maw walked toward Morgan, then looked back at me. "Got a canvas bucket?"

"Why do I need a canvas bucket?"

"To carry the water from the streams. You have to boil it before you drink, or you'll get the Johnny quicksteps."

I grinned at her Southern expression. "Okay, better have one of those, too."

Maw helped Morgan look through the shirts while I shopped for food and the canvas bucket.

When I got back to them, Maw was stroking Morgan's arm. "You're a beautiful girl."

Morgan pulled back and cleared her throat, looking a little uncomfortable. She didn't really like close contact with strangers. She did this thing in large groups where she'd be the first to shake your hand to avoid a hug.

I started humming the song coming from the counter-top radio, "Blowin in the Wind" by Bob Dylan. If I remembered right, Mamma told me that was one of her favorites from the 60s. When Maw rang us up, I noticed she had a couple of small tattoos, but the peace sign on her neck made me think she might have been a flower child from the hippie era.

She totaled the bill, loaded our supplies in a cardboard box, and pushed it across the counter. "Where you going camping?"

"We're heading up to Newfound Gap." The box was heavier than I thought.

"What trail will you be taking?" Maw picked at her teeth with her fingernail.

"The Appalachian Trail past Icewater Spring to the Dry Sluice Gap Trail."

"Oh, that's a beautiful walk. You'll love it. Don't forget to stop at the Sugarlands Visitor Center to get your permit."

"Thanks, Maw. That's our next stop." I gave her a friendly wave.

She returned the courtesy.

CHAPTER 9

THE DRIVE FROM GATLINBURG TO THE SUGARLANDS VISITOR Center to pick up our permits was only a few miles.

Next to me, Morgan rummaged through her purse like a badger clawing dirt.

"What are you looking for?" My low tone held a hint of playful smugness.

She pulled out a hairbrush the size of a mini ping-pong paddle, a small package of tissues, and what appeared to be an empty box of Milk Duds. "My book."

Morgan was meticulous and organized as a dentist, picking around in someone's mouth, but her purse looked like a handbag of giveaway items. "What book?"

"I always take a book when I camp." Her high pitch neared panic as though the book was an integral part of our honeymoon.

I looked across at Morgan and flashed a you-make-me-laugh smile. "What kind of stuff do you read?"

"You mean what genre, don't you?"

"Genre. What's that?"

"Good grief. You probably read books with pictures. You don't read, do you?" Her tone was playful.

"Yes, I do…if someone makes me."

Morgan backhanded my leg.

"Okay, Doctor, what kind of genre do you read?"

"Romance mostly. My favorite author is Jodi Thomas. Her new book is *Mornings on Main*. Oh, there it is on the bottom." Finding the book seemed to relax her.

"I'm surprised you found it in that monster bag. You could lose the Grand Canyon in there."

She closed her eyes, ballooned her cheeks, and exhaled.

I parked the car, and hand-in-hand we walked by the visitor center into the backcountry camping permit office. The walls of the small front office were covered with large topography maps of the park.

"Good morning." A lady, dressed in starched khaki clothes with her brown hair pulled back in a ponytail, greeted us from behind a counter. "I suppose you'd like a camping permit." The lady's name plate read, *Tina Breeze, Park Ranger*. Her name sounded like a fabric softener.

I reached for my money clip. "Yes, what's the price?"

"No charge, but we'd like you to fill out this form with your name and vehicle information."

"I'm Earl Helmsly, and this is my wife Morgan."

The park ranger jotted down our names in what looked like a log book. She looked at our clasped hands. "Are you newlyweds?"

Was it that obvious? "How'd you know?"

"The glow. I've seen it before." Tina reached under the counter and pulled out a map of the hiking areas. "Would you give us your camping location in case of an emergency?"

I released Morgan's hand and pointed to the map. "We're going on the Appalachian Trail past Icewater

Spring, then down Dry Sluice Gap Trail. We'll only be gone two nights."

Tina wrote our plans next to our names. "I'll assume you'll park at Newfound Gap?"

"That's correct."

"I'll make a couple of recommendations. If you see a bear, slowly back away. Black bears aren't usually aggressive, but if there's a cub around, you never know. Don't wander off the trail too far. It's easy to get lost."

I placed my arm around Morgan's waist. "Not going to let her out of my sight for one moment."

"You make a nice-looking couple. Have fun and be safe." Something about the soft look in Tina's eyes as she glanced between us made me wonder if she was reliving a past, pleasant memory.

Tall straight trees hugged the curved road to Newfound Gap. The thirteen-mile drive lasted about thirty minutes and took us through a couple of tunnels that required our lights to be on.

I looked forward to the campout. Just Morgan and me alone. What could be better? I reached over and intertwined my fingers with hers. The next two days were going to be spectacular.

CHAPTER 10

Morgan and I parked in the lot at Newfound Gap and unloaded the camping gear. Before I could get to the tent, she'd strapped it on her back and picked up the butane stove. When I tried to take both, she shook me off. My bride's independence impressed me.

Approaching the sign leading to the Appalachian Trail, Morgan stopped. "Take my picture."

Her pose reminded me of those game show hosts on television, making sweeping motions with her hand, bending one knee, and arching her head back while exposing a row of white teeth so bright it could cause temporary blindness.

"You're such a ham."

The climb eastward on the Appalachian Trail was steady for about two miles, the trail bordered by a wide variety of wildflowers. Morgan said the purple ones were violets. The small blooms were accented by dark green leaves, framing the petals perfectly.

The elevation at the peak of the trail was about six thousand feet. Looking out over the Great Smoky Mountains was heart-stopping. The pale blue sky with puffy, cumulus clouds reminded me of meringue spiked high on the tops of Mamma's cream-filled pies. The ridge of the great mountain looked like the spine of a dinosaur, stripped bare after years of erosion.

Seven miles later, we pitched camp mid-afternoon on a flat area off Dry Sluice Gap Trail. Ravens squawked and chipmunks chattered. The squirrels weren't as friendly. They scampered up the birch trees to a safe place away from the humans.

Morgan set out our meal for dinner, and I tied the rest of our food between two trees over a storage cable someone had left.

Dark seemed to creep up on us. I turned on our lanterns, and we sat on a log and listened to the forest talk. The night bugs had a symphony all their own. The loud chirping relaxed me.

An owl flew over and landed on a large limb above. His loud, monotone hoot startled Morgan. She pulled her legs to her chest, wrapping both arms around them. "Oh, my gosh, that sound sent chills through me. It reminds me of the screeching owls in *The Legend of Sleepy Hollow*."

I picked up a pebble and tossed it at her. "Wimp."

She stuck out her tongue. "I'm going to bed. You're making fun of me." Her slow, hippish walk got my attention. She knew exactly what she was doing, and it worked.

I pushed off the log and grabbed the lantern. "I'm right behind you." I felt a warm closeness to Morgan. My mom, brothers, and sisters were special, but my bride was different. We were united together as one. I'd never experienced anything like it.

When Morgan first suggested a honeymoon in the mountains, I'd hesitated over the non-traditional getaway. Now I realized it was the perfect place to bond and start our life together. No one around but us. No one to interrupt our solitude.

The next morning, I went to the waterfalls below our camp while Morgan stayed behind and started breakfast. I weaved down the mountain to the falls and sat on a rock near the tumbling, rapid water as it cascaded over large gray boulders. I hadn't been there fifteen or twenty minutes when I knew something was wrong. The rain started as I checked my pistol and sprinted up the mountain.

But when I got back to camp, Morgan was gone.

Time stopped. Panic latched on with powerful tentacles. The rain grew heavier, striking the metal frying pan with a loud *ping, ping, ping.*

"Morgan…Morgan, where are you?" I ran to the crumpled tent, lost my balance, and fell forward in the mud. Sharp branches tore my shirt and ripped into my chest. My lungs pounded. My breath rushed out.

Finally, my training kicked in, and I got up. I cocked my P-226 and raised it chest-high, sweeping left, then right.

Think. Think. Morgan's disappearance suffocated me. My hands shook. My lungs filled with fear. Come on, Earl. What's next? Reason it out.

The rain picked up, so intense I could barely see twenty feet in front of me.

I wiped it out of my eyes. Morgan would never walk off alone. There was no evidence of a wild animal attack. No tracks. Nothing. Someone had to have taken her.

Getting to the car and seeking help was the best plan. No time to waste. I had to find her. Had to. I slapped my front pockets searching for the keys. Not there. Where were they? The backpack. Check the backpack inside the tent. No, I'd left the backpack by the dead tree next to the cooking stove.

I tried to unzip it, but my fingers shook so hard I couldn't. Calm down. Calm down. The stiff, metal teeth of the zipper finally parted, and I picked up the bag and dumped everything. The car keys fell out. I scooped them off the ground and ran toward where we'd left the car at Newfound Gap.

Pace yourself. Run steady. Don't use all your energy. A SEAL who can't function under pressure is a useless SEAL. I had to be calm for Morgan.

I focused on my mission — get back to the Ranger Station — while I pieced the puzzle together. Morgan had gotten up at 7:30 before I left for the falls. I got back to camp at 7:50. Twenty friggin' minutes. Why didn't I try to get Morgan to go with me? Why didn't I make her keep the pistol with her? My fault. My mistake.

The trail was a river of mud. I slipped, catching myself before sliding off the path into dense undergrowth. Keep running. Pace yourself.

I reached the car at 11:30 and sped out of the parking area, narrowly missing a car coming into the lot. Thank God the rain slowed enough for the windshield wipers to do their job. Even then, it took me twenty-five minutes to reach the visitor center. Twenty-five minutes too long. I slammed on the brakes, opened the door, and sprinted into the permit office.

CHAPTER 11

WHEN I RUSHED INSIDE THE BUILDING, TINA STOOD UP FROM behind the reception counter, one hand cupped over her mouth. Her gaze froze on me as though she knew something had happened.

"Morgan's missing." I swiped the rain from my hair while trying to catch my breath.

Tina's body stiffened as she cleared her throat. "Mrs. Helmsly? She's lost?"

I slammed my fist onto the counter. "No, someone took her. She's been kidnapped." My voice hardened, tight with fear and chocked with panic.

Tina started shaking as she stepped back from the counter and rushed to the back of the building.

Not a minute later, a large man with coal black hair and a heavy, bristly mustache dressed in a ranger uniform approached me. "Mr. Helmsly, I'm Leroy Shannon." He shook my hand. "Please follow me."

I walked behind him into his office.

"Have a seat." He motioned to one of the two metal chairs against the wall. "Tell me what happened."

I pulled up a chair to his desk but couldn't sit. "She's gone. She's just gone." My mouth filled with the metallic taste of adrenaline, my head light from the run and lack of food. "I went to the waterfall. I wasn't gone more than twenty minutes." I paced in front of the ranger's desk. "Someone took her."

Shannon maneuvered to sit behind the desk, his large legs scraping the corner. "Are you sure it wasn't an animal attack, Mr. Helmsly? Or maybe she just went for a hike?"

"The tent was knocked over, the food was scattered, and there were no signs of an animal. Morgan would never wander off alone. She's an experienced camper." I gripped the back of the chair. "You have to do something. We have to find her. You have to help me."

"And I will, Mr. Helmsly. We'll send a search team." He tapped a pen on his metal desk, the sound adding to my stress. "But if we're going to find her, I need more information."

"Fine." I squeezed the chair harder. The faster this conversation went, the faster we could get out there and look for my wife.

"Did you and the missus have a spat this morning?" Something in Shannon's tone made it sound less like information gathering and more like an interrogation.

"No." I let go of the chair.

"How long have you been married?"

"Why is that important?" My blood wasn't boiling, but close.

"Take it easy." This time his tone was softer. "I'm just trying to get as many facts as I can that will help us."

I took a deep breath and exhaled, trying to compose myself. "We've been married three days. This is our honeymoon. I may as well tell you now, I have a pistol. I offered it to Morgan before I went to the waterfall, but she said she wouldn't need it."

"Do you have the firearm on you now?" The ranger gave me an uneasy look.

"It's in my car, under the driver's side seat."

"And it hasn't been fired?"

"No." I didn't like the direction he was going. "What are you getting at? You think I had something to do with her disappearance?"

"I didn't say that. But I've been a park ranger for eighteen years and been involved in dozens of rescue searches. Not one of them was a kidnapping." He had a puzzled look on his face as if he was trying to think of a kidnapping anywhere in a national park.

"Look." I finally sat in the chair. "You can think whatever you want about me. But please, just help me find my wife. We're wasting time."

"I need to check in with the District Ranger, Larry Hauser." Shannon reached for the phone and punched in some numbers. "Larry? Leroy Shannon. A man just walked into my office and reported his wife missing. He claims she was kidnapped this morning from the park. Tina will fax you the incident report with his personal information. Can you line up a search team for tomorrow?"

"Tomorrow?" I jumped out of the chair. "Tomorrow could be too late."

He held up his hand to quiet me and kept talking. "The Helmslys were camping in a remote area. I'm taking him and my dog back to the mountain to do a preliminary search and pinpoint the location of the disappearance.

I'll get back to you when we return." He hung up the phone, pushed it aside, and stood up. "Give me thirty minutes to go get Jake, my bloodhound, and we'll go back to the campsite."

Throat tight, I nodded, completely insecure and helpless.

Shannon tugged on his pants. "The park has a least a hundred people we can call into service. That includes the Air National Guard along with the Gatlinburg Fire Department."

"Dogs? What about dogs? Is Jake the only one available?"

He shook his head and scratched the back of his neck. Veins protruded down the side of his forehead. "No. Jake's my personal dog. We outsource other dogs with the use of a data base." Shannon walked to a table adjacent to the door and picked up two walkie-talkies. He handed me one. "Keep this with you. Everyone on the rescue team will have one to communicate. The park has its own frequency so no interference is possible." Shannon snapped a walkie-talkie onto his belt. "Do you have any of your wife's clothes with you?"

"She left one of her suitcases in the car."

He shoved his pen and a pad of paper at me. "While I'm gone, write down everything you can remember about last night and this morning, including the time sequence, then get some of her clothes. Don't be alarmed if the initial search group that sets out in the morning is small. Fewer people will not disturb the area as much. It's raining in the mountains too?" He looked at my wet, muddy clothes.

I managed to raise my head and give a weak nod.

"I hope the rain didn't wash away the scent or the foot prints." Shannon looked down, eyes locked on the tile floor.

I couldn't tell whether he was planning his next move or giving up before we got started. My legs shook, my stomach filled with acid, and my chest tied in bowline knots. Memories of Morgan took over my thoughts — meeting her in the dental chair, her walking down the aisle, standing in the door at the Eckland Motel on our wedding night. So many memories. Too many to count. My mind and body merged into a bundle of numbness.

How could our honeymoon have begun in heaven only to end in hell?

CHAPTER 12

I FINISHED THE INCIDENT REPORT AND PUSHED IT ACROSS Shannon's desk. While I waited for him to return with his bloodhound, I went limp in the metal chair and stared out the window.

If something happened to Morgan, I wouldn't survive. In the time she'd been part of my life, she'd become my world. Being without her would pull me into a pit I might never climb out of. I couldn't live without her.

Unable to sit still any longer, I pushed away from the desk and headed out to get the suitcase she'd left in the car.

"Can I get you something to drink, Mr. Helmsly?" Tina asked as I passed the front counter.

I shook my heavy head and shuffled across the lot, kicking up bits of gravel. The closer I got to the car, the more anxiety latched on. I unlocked the trunk and opened it. Seeing her suitcase pulled me toward a very dark place.

A pickup with a camper pulled in front of the permit office. Shannon got out, opened the shell, and a blond dog jumped out. The harnessed bloodhound was huge. His powerful shoulder muscles flexed with each step. The dog headed toward me. Shannon pulled back on the leash. "When Jake's in his harness, he knows it's time to go to work."

I grabbed Morgan's luggage and followed Jake and Shannon back into the building.

Tina met us and gave Shannon what looked like a folded sheet. He spread the cloth in the middle of the chipped, green concrete floor. "Your wife's clothes will go here. Jake'll pull up her smell."

I opened the suitcase and reached inside for her clothes.

Shannon grabbed my hand and shook his head. "Dump them out. Don't touch 'em. We don't want your scent mixed with Morgan's."

The dog lowered his head, sucked in air through his long snout, then exhaled. He went to every item of clothing. When finished, he raised his big, oblong head and looked at Shannon as though he was ready to go. He showed no emotion. No hint of excitement. He was all business. And he could be the key to locating Morgan.

We locked eyes briefly. It was as though he knew I was connected to the person he would be searching for. I prayed he could do the job.

We pulled out of Sugarlands Visitor Center in Shannon's pickup truck and headed back to Newfound Gap. The windshield wipers pushed away the flood of water.

Going back to our campsite would be a major challenge, one I didn't know if I could handle. An imaginary rope looped around my chest, crushing me with panic.

Last night Morgan and I were together. Happy and in love forever. Today, I was in a pickup with a man and a dog searching for my future.

"Would you like to know how the search will progress?" Shannon broke the silence.

"Yes." My barely audible voice fractured.

"You did the right thing coming to me. You would've wasted valuable time trying to locate Morgan on your own."

I wanted to bring up all the valuable time we spent in his office while he accused me of having something to do with her disappearance, but I tightened my jaw instead.

"Jake's a good dog." Shannon turned the wipers up a notch. "He's found many lost people in the park. He's relentless. Once followed a smell for six miles in a search-and-rescue mission a few years back. If he gets a strong hit, he won't quit."

A jolt of optimism rocked me. I turned toward Shannon. "That's good news, and I need some good news."

He slowly nodded and gave me a look that said, *Jake and I've got your back.*

For the first time today, I had a glimmer of hope. I straightened and leaned forward in the truck. "I haven't thanked you for all you've done."

Shannon took his hand off the steering wheel and waved it back and forth like he was uncomfortable with my gratitude. "I promise you, the search team and I will not stop until every effort has been made to find Morgan. It's one thing to look for a lost person, but a probable kidnapping... those SOBs. Nothing will make me happier than to bring them to justice."

A sliver of light pushed its way through the bluish-gray clouds as we pulled into the parking lot at Newfound Gap, and the rain stopped.

Jake clawed at the pickup bed like he was anxious to get started, his enthusiasm contagious.

Shannon opened the tailgate, grabbed the leash, and Jake jumped out, immediately heading to the Appalachian Trail.

"Shannon, how did he know to head out on this trail?"

"He's been here before. This is the starting point for many backcountry outings."

I had to fast-walk to keep up with the dog that never raised his head. "Why doesn't he sniff the air?"

"Bloodhounds pick up scent from the ground. You need a different dog for the air."

"What kind of dogs are those?"

"German Shepherds or Border Collies. Those dogs will be here tomorrow. If Morgan brushed against a tree or put her hand on a boulder, the scent will remain for a while."

I grabbed Shannon's arm and turned him toward me. Our eyes met. "You said something about the rain washing away traces of Morgan earlier."

Shannon stroked his heavy, black mustache. "I'll be honest. It depends on how heavy the rain fell. Water can make it difficult for the dogs."

A hollowness in my chest slowed my breathing, and a shiver ricocheted down my back. "Are you telling me we could've lost Morgan's scent, and we may never find her?" I raked both hands through my hair and clasp them behind my head, not wanting to hear his answer.

"No, I'm saying the rain could wash away the initial scent, but it doesn't mean the dog can't pick it up again if we're in the right location." He placed a reassuring hand on my shoulder.

His calmness relaxed me. I nodded and exhaled. "Sorry. I'm not familiar with civilian search-and-rescue tactics." Stop doubting, Earl. The man's doing everything he can to help.

He removed his hand. "It's okay."

We'd walked about two hundred yards on the hiking trail when something got Jake's attention, and he pulled off. His muscular body jerked hard on the leash, his powerful legs moving forward in the wet undergrowth.

Could it be Morgan's scent? A chill spiraled through my body. My gaze froze on the dog.

"Earl, did you pull off the trail here yesterday?"

"No, and we're not even close to the campsite."

"Did Morgan relieve herself in this area?"

I shook my head. "No."

Shannon pointed toward the bushes where something moved. "It could be a wild boar. That's about the only thing that distracts Jake. Let's move on."

The trek to the campsite was a muddy mess, but Jake never broke stride once the boar incident passed.

About seven miles later, I gnawed the inside of my cheek and gave a hard tug on Shannon's starched uniform sleeve. "Our camp...just ahead."

The air hung thick and heavy like soup — the sight of the camp surreal as though I'd never been there before, but at the same time never left. I dropped to one knee, my heart breaking into pieces thinking of my bride and what she was going through. Images flashed in front of me so horrible I had to erase them from my conscience.

"Are you okay?" Shannon's tone was soft with a touch of southern kindness I hadn't noticed before.

I wasn't okay at all, but I gave him a quick nod.

"Walk carefully around the area. Look for anything that might be helpful to the search team but don't touch anything."

I went to the tent. Morgan's brush lay by the collapsed structure. I started to pick it up but remembered Shannon's instructions.

"Earl." His baritone voice got my attention. "Come here."

I turned around.

Jake's nose was plastered to the ground.

"We've got something." Shannon snapped his fingers.

CHAPTER 13

THE LAST TIME I SAW MORGAN IN THE CAMPGROUND, SHE WAS tying an orange bandana around her head as she said, "Bye." The vision hit me like jolts of electricity. My eyes twitched, and I couldn't focus.

"Earl, did you hear me?" Shannon asked. "We've got something." Shannon and Jake were both staring intently at the ground.

Their concentrated attention stopped my heart, then the beats came pounding back so powerful I felt them in my neck. I rushed to the spot. "Morgan's wedding ring." I covered my mouth to keep from screaming. Bending on one knee, I reached for the diamond then realized there might be prints other than Morgan's and mine.

Shannon picked up the ring with a small twig and placed it in a baggie. He stood and looked around. "Jake, go on boy. See what you can find." He loosened the grip on the leash. The dog's nose pulled to the ground, sweeping left, then right through the green foliage and brown dirt.

The bloodhound reminded me of a metal detector testing the ground for hidden treasures, but material treasure was nothing compared to Morgan. If he locked onto her scent, it could mean the difference between life and death.

I stayed back and to the side of Jake, not wanting to invade his work space, but I did follow his every move. A stress headache pounded behind my eyes. My jaw tightened like a steel cable.

Shannon worked Jake for another hour, mostly in the camp area, and the bloodhound didn't pick up a scent. "It's not unusual to come up short the first day. I know you're frustrated and disappointed, Earl. Your empty stare's a blueprint for how you must feel. We'll get a full team tomorrow. Don't give up hope. The best dogs and the best handlers in the business will get an early start."

There was something about his voice that was genuine, and I believed him.

The drive back to his office was quiet. My mind flipped from the search to calling Morgan's mom. What would I say to her? What could I possibly say?

CHAPTER 14

I COULDN'T CAMP, NOT WITHOUT MORGAN, SO I RENTED A condo in Gatlinburg at the Laurel Inn. Not knowing how long I'd be there, I explained my story to Linda, the lady at the front desk. She was very helpful and said the unit would be available as long as I needed it.

I opened the condo door, laid the key on the kitchen counter, and stared at the telephone. Exhaustion was an understatement. My legs felt like they'd been beaten with a rubber hose. My mind pin-balled on how to tell Melody. Taking a dagger to my heart would be easier than telling her Morgan was missing.

Think, Earl. Think before you call. Try to be calm.

I sat on the blue-and-white pinstriped sofa next to the table that held the phone and rubbed my sweaty palms on my pant legs. My hand shook reaching for the receiver.

I couldn't do it.

I pushed off the sofa, went to the sink, and turned on the cold water and cupped it, then splashed it on my face. I pounded my fist onto the counter and looked back at the phone. No, it wasn't fair to Melody. I had to call her. It was the right thing to do. I returned to the couch, picked up the phone and dialed. One ring, two, then a third.

"Hello." Melody finally answered.

I didn't want to talk.

"Hello?" Melody asked. "Is anyone there?"

A wall mirror across the room reflected my disgusting and dirty image. I should've showered. "Melody."

"Earl, how's the honeymoon? Are you two having the time of your life? I've been thinking about you all day. Let me talk with Morgan. I bet—"

"Melody, something happened." I cut her off.

I could hear her surprised breath, then she cleared her throat. "What is it?"

I wanted to run out the door, get in my car, and never come back. But I had to tell her. "Morgan's missing. This morning I went to a waterfall below our camp. She stayed behind to make breakfast. When I returned, she was gone."

"Gone? What do you mean gone?" Her high-pitched voice filled with anger. "What'd you let happen to my baby? Boy, you tell me. Tell me now."

I bent over and rocked back and forth on the sofa. I cried, but no sound came out. "Someone took her." My voice trembled as the words dropped off my tongue.

CHAPTER 15

THE NEXT MORNING, WHEN I PULLED INTO THE SUGARLANDS Visitor Center parking lot, I spotted Melody's car. Seeing her vehicle took my breath. I'd faced challenges in my SEAL career, but nothing came close to admitting my failure to take care of my wife.

Unfolding my tired body from behind the wheel was tough. Lack of sleep made me feel like I had a hangover when I'd had nothing to drink. At least I was clean. I'd stood under the shower last night until the hot water ran out. Then I stood under it longer. Until my body shook with cold.

I walked past the reception desk down the hall to Shannon's office. Melody sat at an angle in front of Leroy's desk. Her hair was a mess and her clothes were wrinkled. I stopped at the door just as she looked up. For a nanosecond, my eyes met hers, then too ashamed to face her, I glanced down.

Shannon slid past me and went behind his desk. "Ma'am, Leroy Shannon with the Park Ranger Service."

Melody extended her hand, and it disappeared between his large, thick palms. "Melody Whitten." Moisture filled her weary eyes, but she forced an awkward, crooked smile.

"Could I get you something to drink, Melody?" The ranger rubbed the back of his neck as though he'd had a restless night.

"Tina's bringing some water. " She moved a worn, brown leather purse from her lap to the floor.

Leroy tucked his chin and looked up at me with half-lid eyes. "Would you and Melody like some time?"

I'd rather face an enemy with an AK-47, but I stepped back to let him by, then took his place behind the desk.

Melody straightened in her chair to face me. If looks could kill, I was halfway in the grave. Her lips stretched into a long, thin line, her chin quivering as though she was struggling to hang on. "What happened?" Her tone cut across the question sharper than a barber's razor.

My hands shook. "I woke early and decided to go down to a waterfall below camp." My voice was timid and humble. "Morgan didn't want to go. She stayed behind to get breakfast ready." I tensed, not knowing how Melody would react. "I offered to leave a pistol, but she refused. I was at the falls about twenty minutes. When I got back to camp, Morgan was gone." Tears rivered down my cheek, the pain so intense it was as though a thousand ice picks plunged into my soul.

Melody pressed on the edge of the desk and stood. "Come around here." Her voice was low.

The demand caught me off guard. "What?"

"Come around here." This time the command was crystal clear.

I pushed back from the desk, the chair rollers squeaking on the linoleum floor. I had no idea what to expect, but if Melody wanted to smack me around, she had every right.

We stood face-to-face for what seemed like hours. Then she placed her gnarled fingers on my shoulders and squeezed. "Son, I've had a long drive to think about my reaction on the phone. I handled it badly. You had nothing to do with this." Her voice went from stern to sweet. "Don't beat yourself down for what happened. Let me tell you something about Morgan."

My rigid, tense body relaxed.

Her eyes, while still sad almost seemed to sparkle. "Those fools who took her — and I say fools plural because no one man on this mountain could do it by himself — are in for a big surprise. My girl's a fighter. When Morgan was seven, she didn't come home for lunch one day. I didn't worry too much. I figured she ate at Michelle's house. About three that afternoon, I called her mom. She said Morgan had lunch and headed home after the girls practiced their duet for church Sunday. I called everywhere, went everywhere, even got the police looking for her. About six o'clock in the evening the fire department found her stuck in a drainage pipe. She'd crawled in chasing after a kitten. The first words out of her mouth were, 'Got any purple Kool-Aid? I'm thirsty.' Morgan's tough. She'll be alright. You got my word on that. We just gotta find her."

It was clear where Morgan got her strength and character. Feeling like a ton of coal had been lifted off my shoulders, I wrapped both arms around Melody and pulled her close.

CHAPTER 16

LEROY SHANNON ASKED MELODY AND ME TO MEET HIM AT THE park ranger station behind the visitor center in thirty minutes to give us details about the search and answer our questions. I took the meeting to be similar to a SEAL briefing before a mission.

Even though it was a parking lot away, I drove us there in her car. For August, the weather was damp, foggy, and cold. Street lights pierced the morning mist with a blood-orange glow and made me feel alone and frightened. Thinking about Morgan and whatever horrors she faced destroyed me. I wanted to kill the people responsible.

Melody said very little during the short drive. Only God knew what a mother went through at a time like this. But I knew what I was thinking, and it wasn't good.

The parking lot at the station was half full. Shannon's pickup caught my attention. I stopped the car, got out, and helped Melody. We had to buzz in before the door was opened.

A slim, striking lady greeted us. "Are you here to see Mr. Shannon?" Her strong southern accent was warm and friendly.

"Yes." My voice monotone and flat.

She pointed down a long, dimly lit hallway. "I'll take you back. Would you like some coffee?"

Melody nodded. "That would be nice."

I shook my head. "No, thank you." Coffee first thing in the morning without eating made me sick at times — didn't want to risk it today.

The woman went to the coffee pot and got Melody a cup. "Will you please follow me?"

We trailed behind her down the hall. The stiffness in Melody's walk could have been an arthritis flare up. I hoped the distance wasn't too far for her.

Two chairs were set up side-by-side in front of a desk. Melody set her coffee on a coaster and took the closest seat to Shannon.

He stood and greeted us. "I have a pretty good idea what you're going through. We'll do everything in our power to make you as comfortable as possible." He moved what looked like a large folded map to the corner of the desk and sat. He gestured for me to sit as well. "The Incident Command Center will be set up in a training room across the hall. We'll meet every morning to discuss the searches, trails, and logistics. I'll assign a family liaison to keep you updated. We'll let you know the plan for the day and give you as much information as we have at regular intervals. Do you have any other family here?"

"My family's coming today." Burl, Tony, Mary Nelle, and Belinda were bringing Mamma. Family support was welcomed and needed.

"Do you have any questions?" Shannon's confident air gave me confidence.

"My family will want to assist in the search," I told him. "Will we be going with you?"

Shannon leaned back, his hands clasped over the ends of the chair arms. He fixed a strong gaze on me. "You coming is not allowed." His tone was polite but professional.

"I can't search for my wife?" My question came with a hard edge. "You took me yesterday. What's the difference?" My heart, two ticks away from busting out of my chest, was saying no way was I staying back.

"Yesterday was different. I needed you to direct me to the exact location. Remember me telling you not to disturb things?" Shannon's crisp voice was direct and to the point. There was no question he was in charge. "We've got this."

It had a calming effect, but my heart still pounded against my rib cage.

"Let me explain." He paused, seemingly to gather his thoughts. "Trained observers will notice signs such as a broken tree limb that's fresh. They'll pick up on a footprint that's not visible to most people or a moss-covered rock with the slime disturbed by someone's foot. It's not that we don't want your help, but you and your family haven't been trained in search-and-rescue techniques. And I'll tell you, Earl, too many people looking in a given area can really foul up our plan. We're much more efficient when the area isn't contaminated with extra footprints. The search area of the park has been closed to all visitors to prevent this. It's important you understand."

Melody looked like she was still in shock as she nodded.

It was hard to concede, but he had a point. Morgan deserved the best chance. I sank back already exhausted, and the day was just beginning.

"How many people will be involved in the search?" Melody asked.

"No more than twenty-four with two canine units."

"What about choppers?" I shifted in my chair.

"An overhead unit will be used. I'll go into more details later. Like I said, every day we'll keep you updated."

How many days was he talking? I stared at the metal desk. The light from the green-shaded lamp mesmerized me. Could I even handle one more day without Morgan?

CHAPTER 17

Sleep evaded me for the second straight night. Yesterday's search found nothing. The what-ifs and guilt devoured me like a disease. I needed answers soon, or there was a good chance insanity might latch on and refuse to let go.

Melody, Mamma, my brothers and sisters, and I arrived at the ranger station before sunup to meet the park service family liaison. The canine teams and handlers were already in place, the yelping dogs eager to begin.

Wall maps, walkie-talkies, and flashlights were stockpiled in the training room. The aroma of freshly brewed coffee made me nauseated. Several overhead fluorescent lights flickered on and off. The room reminded me of the alien movie *The Thing*.

While my family sat at two eight-foot tables, Mamma and Melody next to each other, I paced around the room.

Melody rocked back and forth on the metal chair, her eyes wide and fixed like she was staring, but what was she seeing?

Mamma patted Melody's hand and just kept shaking her head.

At 8:10, the door finally opened. Shannon and a tall, slender man approached us.

I pulled up a chair and sat at the end of the tables.

"Good morning." Shannon laid a pair of binoculars and a clipboard next to me. "I want to introduce Norvelle Holvachek." Stepping back, he gestured toward the stranger. "He'll be your family liaison."

Holvachek adjusted his round, wire-framed glasses and pulled on the cuffs of his starched park-service shirt. He looked more like a classical music composer than a liaison officer. "Good morning. My responsibility is to keep you updated on the search and let you know the plans for the day. You may ask me questions at any time. If I don't know the answer, I'll find out and get back to you as soon as possible."

I imagined my family before this — happy and enjoying life — and I hated myself for what I allowed to happen.

Holvachek pulled out a metal chair from the tables and sat. "I won't pretend to know exactly what you're going through, but I'm familiar with Mr. Shannon and the search teams. They're top-notch professionals who are dedicated to finding Morgan." He hesitated, removing his glasses and rubbing the bridge of his nose before replacing them. "The park classifies this as an emergency. A high priority. I'll remain in contact with you every day until the last search team returns." His calm, professional manner was exactly what I needed.

Norvelle turned to me. "With your permission, Morgan's picture and description will be distributed to news sources and the police."

I nodded. "Of course."

He continued. "Are there any questions?"

"Will we be able to stay here during the day?" Melody spoke first.

"No." Holvachek shook his head. "I've checked with the Laurel Inn. There's a conference room at that location where you can all wait together."

Mamma stood. "I'm Earl's mamma, Glynna Helmsly. Is there anything we can do to help the search teams?"

He thought for a second and then said, "Food would be appreciated for members of the search teams."

"The Laurel Inn has a smoker by the pool." She seemed to relax a little now that she had something to do. "I'll cook a brisket and pork shoulder."

"You can bring sack lunches to the ranger station before the teams leave in the mornings."

Shannon stepped up. "The search team is about ready to head to Newfound Gap. Please go to the Laurel Inn. Mr. Holvachek will meet you there. I'll keep in touch with him."

Norvelle stood. "Shannon, I'd like to speak with you before we go." The two walked to the door and left the training room.

CHAPTER 18

D<small>AY</small> <small>THREE OF THE SEARCH, THE FAMILY GATHERED IN THE</small> Laurel Inn's conference room for supper. Mary Nelle and Belinda got on my nerves, their high-pitched voices echoing off the pale yellow walls. Burl and Tony grumbled over who got the last Sprite.

I knew they wanted to help but — I took a sip of water from a paper cup, my throat as tight as the mounting tension.

Melody separated herself from the group and sat at the far end of the room, regressing by the hour, the fight I'd seen in her that first day dying by the second. Sadness seemed to reach into her posture, hunching her shoulders, weighing her down. But the worst was the hollow look in her eyes that reflected the hopelessness in mine.

I caused that. And it cut me to the core. To make matters worse, there was some part of Shannon that still suspected me. Yesterday, after the family meeting, I passed his office and overheard him tell Holvachek, "I like the guy, truly do, but you never know what someone's capable of. All too often, the person closest to the victim's guilty." He followed that up by asking Tina if my background check had come in yet.

When it did, he'd find out about my service record. And about all the time I spent locked in the brig over bar brawls. My commanding officer used to say my temper was a mark against me. But those eight or nine bar fights weren't my fault. The yellow-dog Marines had no right to talk down about the Navy. I was justified in punching their clocks. Any loyal Navy man would stand up for his uniform. I had no animosity toward the jarheads. They just needed a little attitude adjustment. But Shannon might not take it that way. He might see a schizoid who couldn't control his emotions — who would hurt his own wife.

Stupid, Earl. You were stupid then. You're stupid now. I kicked at the air as though that would help. My short temper almost cost me the SEAL program. And it could taint Shannon's opinion of me. I needed him on my side. But I had no clue how to convince him of my innocence. I wadded up the empty paper cup and slammed it into the trash can.

The blasted walkie-talkie squeaked and crackled.

I cranked the volume down, annoyed with its incessant garble and lack of news, clipped it to my waist, and headed outside away from the suffocating asylum at the inn.

Someone tapped me on the shoulder. "Hey, brother."

The richness of Tony's deep bass voice reminded me how much I'd appreciated and admired him as a father figure. "Let's walk. I need to stretch my legs."

"Sure." I exhaled. "I'd like the company."

We left the Laurel Inn and headed down a long flight of wooden stairs that led to downtown Gatlinburg. The evening sun warmed my battle-weary face. I took a deep breath of cool mountain air, trying to calm my frustration.

People at the outdoor pubs we passed laughed and joked. They were enjoying a normal evening out while I was waist-deep in my own personal hell—living in a world without Morgan. Envy and resentment made my jaw rock hard.

Tony placed a big right hand around my shoulder and squeezed, pulling me close to his side. "Life's not fair, and I don't know how all of this is going to work out, but you have your family, and we'll always be with you."

I hung my head.

"Always." Tony squeezed my shoulder again. "I don't have any magic words to comfort you. All I can do is be here for you. This isn't your fault. The blame goes to the SOBs who took her. Wherever Morgan is, she's thinking about you. Be strong for her." His voice resonated confidence. "We all love you, man."

My tension-tight jaw relaxed.

"If you were separated from your team on a SEAL mission, what would you do?" Tony asked.

I stopped to face him. "Find my way back."

Tony grabbed the back of my neck and squeezed. "And what would your team do?"

"They'd wait. They'd never leave without me." I'd allowed defeat to take hold. That's not who I was, and it wasn't who Morgan was either.

Tony nodded. "That's the mindset you need about Morgan. I can't explain it, but if you don't, she'll know. Do you hear me, Earl? She...will...know."

He was right. I wasn't sure when I'd fallen into such a dark hole, but I did know I had to climb out, and I'd better start right now. I gave Tony a man-hug.

He followed me to the conference room, and we called the family together.

"I've got something to say." I waited for their complete attention. "We've got two options... give up on ever seeing Morgan again or get our minds right and be positive. Every waking moment from now on I'll be thinking of when we'll be together again. If we don't believe we'll find her, she'll sense it and give up."

Melody pushed her tired, arthritic body out of her chair. "You're right. I've said before Morgan's a fighter. And look at us. We've given up. Well, not anymore. Not me. I ain't givin' up." Her body grew straight. "My daughter's strong. I know she's looking for ways to escape. Don't doubt that for a moment." Her words acted like a powder keg to our spirits.

Positive vibes filled the room. Everyone hugged each other, and the beginnings of what might be smiles returned.

I looked at Tony. "Thank you." I couldn't love the guy any more.

He wrapped his big arms around me and whispered, "Trust the Lord. He knows your pain, and He's with you. Just trust Him and pray."

My walkie-talkie buzzed. I stepped out of the room and turned up the volume.

"Earl, can you hear me?" It was Shannon.

"Loud and clear," I spoke into the mic.

"Does Morgan have an orange University of Tennessee bandana?"

"Yes, she had it on when I went to the falls."

"We found one." Shannon's voice crackled over the speaker.

Thirty minutes ago, I felt like I'd been sucked down a drainage pipe and impaled on a grate, but the bandana pulled me out, wiped me off, and gave me new life. "It has to be hers."

"My bloodhound agrees." A hint of hope replaced the monotone drone he normally used with me.

We would find Morgan. We had to.

CHAPTER 19

Waiting for Holvachek's daily five o'clock briefing would take too long. I needed to see Shannon now.

I got out of my car at the ranger station feeling like a breaker box overloaded with Christmas lights.

Shannon's dog watched me through the window of the camper shell. As I walked toward the pickup, Jake barked, not a warning bark, but a bark that seemed to say he found something for me. Something I'd like. He scratched on the pickup bed like he was summoning me—*come here, come here, come here.*

The camper shell window was open. Jake noticed me. His tongue lolled to one side, bouncing up and down, his teeth shining. If dogs could smile, he just did.

I grasped his large, blond head with both hands and gave a brisk rub. "Thanks, buddy. You did good today."

He barked on cue as though he understood.

I left Jake barking with his head sticking out the window, nose turned up. An alpha dog, for sure. He'd have made a great SEAL. I headed to Leroy's office.

He met me at the door. The half-cocked smile beneath his Teddy Roosevelt mustache gave me hope. He reached out with his puffy, speckled right hand. "Have a seat,

Earl." He moved to the chair behind his desk and pulled a plastic baggie from a manila envelope.

Morgan's orange bandana.

Excitement bounced around my chest like a pinball. I dove for the baggie.

Shannon raised his hand. "Don't take it out. We haven't checked for prints."

I gently touched the plastic. It was as though Morgan was in the room with me. I pictured her sticking her head out of the tent wearing the bandana the last time I saw her.

"We found the bandana about a hundred-and-fifty yards northeast of your campsite," he said. "We'll concentrate our efforts in that direction."

I held my breath, almost afraid to speak. "This is good news, right?"

Shannon nodded as though he'd seen the hurt etched on my face and knew the scarf was more than a piece of cloth to me. He carefully took back the baggie with the bandana and tucked it back into the envelope.

My empty hands fractured my heart. For a split-second it stopped, the pain so sharp I didn't know if the beats would pick up again.

Shannon leaned forward and placed his elbows on the desk.

Why did I know his next words would stomp me like a rodeo bull?

He took time interlocking his fingers like he needed another moment. "There is one thing. We found no other signs of human activity."

I winced. "What does that mean?"

"I don't know yet. We have to hang tight. There could've been more clues, but it was almost dark. We'll know more tomorrow."

Getting a bad feeling, I leaned forward over his desk. "Shoot it to me straight."

"The bandana could be a diversion. It looked planted to me...out in the open, too obvious. "

I sagged in the chair like a worn-out cushion. He might as well have picked up a two-by-four and buried it in my skull. Minutes ago I had hope, but hope came with more than the power to heal. It carried the power to crush. Hope could be the cruelest thing in the world.

I slapped his desk with an open palm, pushed back against the chair, sent it crashing into the wall, and walked out.

"Earl, come back," Shannon called after me. "I could be wrong about the bandana."

I got in my car and slammed the door so hard the windows rattled. Who had my wife? What were they doing to her? Would I ever see her again? The positive outlook I'd had earlier evaporated quicker than rain on a hot August tarmac in Memphis.

I looked at the ranger station. The gray building, highlighted by bluish-green lights on poles and flood lamps on the corners, reminded me of a prison. Whether I drove away or not, I couldn't get free of the bars that kept me locked away from Morgan.

CHAPTER 20

I TURNED MY LOUNGE CHAIR TOWARD THE WINDOW IN MY condo and watched daylight break over the mountain. Leaves swayed back and forth on a group of birch trees huddled together, scattering the golden light in all directions. Outside, all was calm and peaceful. Inside, I was a twisted mass of nerves.

The morning meeting with Holvachek would be different today. Shannon would accompany him. That was an omen. A bad omen. It had been fourteen days since Morgan's kidnapping. The roiling acid in my gut told me they were going to call off the search. Didn't they know living without Morgan would leave me barren as a dried lake bed?

My walk to the conference room felt like a trek through wet concrete — each step sluggish and weighted — as I walked into an emotional ambush I couldn't avoid. I didn't want to see the rangers. I didn't want to hear their excuses. I didn't want to go home without my wife.

At 8:55, I slid into the seat next to Melody at a table in the middle of the room. Slumped in the chairs behind us, Mary Nelle and Belinda reminded me of zombies with their slack faces and beaten-down bodies. Burl leaned forward on his metal chair, elbows on his knees, eyes angled up at the clock. It was as though he had a bad feeling about today's meeting. The tension stacked so thick you could cut it with a butcher's knife. Fear didn't have a recognizable odor, but I still smelled it.

At exactly 9:00, Shannon and Holvachek joined us. Shannon leaned against the wall, almost separating himself from the group, but Holvachek made his way directly to our table. Professional walk. Crisp uniform. The liaison officer had no place for wrinkles on his clothes or scuffs on his boots. They were spit-shine polished, so smooth the ceiling light reflected off the toes. He adjusted his glasses. "May I sit?" He gestured toward the chair across from Melody and me.

Melody pushed her gnarled fingers back and forth across the wrinkled table cloth—a nervous reaction I'd seen before—then nodded and clasped her hands over her mouth as if to hold back her emotions.

I crossed my arms over my chest.

Holvachek made direct eye contact as if he thought he needed to get our attention, but he'd had it as soon as he'd walked into the room. "I wish I didn't have to tell you this. The search inside the park has been called off." Before I could argue, he lifted his index finger.

"That's not to say the search has been abandoned. The FBI will continue looking for Morgan. Fliers with her picture have been placed on every trailhead, at the visitor centers, and gas stations. The television networks all over Tennessee have and will continue to do telecasts."

Hating that my instincts had been right, I pounded the table with my fist. Holvachek might as well have gutted me like an Easter hog. I looked at Shannon, who was motionless, plastered against the wall. "It's only been fourteen days. That's not enough. Keep the search going. That's your job."

Shannon raised both hands, palms out. "I understand your anger, Earl, but here's the problem. The dog teams come from all over the state. Some have been called to other locations. Without more evidence, we can't keep them here."

I sagged in my chair, throwing my head back before looking at Shannon again. "That's a bunch of BS. You're telling me, if it was *your* wife, you'd just give up and call off the search. I don't think so."

"If something comes up and new evidence is found, we'll start again." Holvachek wrung his hands.

"Let me reemphasize that the passive search will continue." Shannon walked toward our table. "People will hear the broadcasts and see the fliers. The FBI looks at a kidnapping differently than someone lost in the park. Kidnapping is a criminal act."

"Then why stop now? Keep looking until the FBI takes charge." My sharp-as-a-buzz saw tone spewed as rage built in me like a pressure cooker. It was all I could do to keep from grabbing both rangers and cracking their collective numbskulls together.

"You can't stop looking." Tony stood and pushed his chair to the side. "This is wrong."

"This ain't right," Burl echoed.

Holvachek turned toward Shannon, his body as stiff as his starched shirt. No emotion, he was a professional robot. "I'll let Ranger Shannon close out. He'll answer any additional questions you have." Holvachek walked to the door and left.

"This whole search has been a joke," Mary Nelle said, without getting up from her chair.

Shannon stepped closer to our table. "Please, let me explain. This is hard on everyone. Maybe it will help if you let me show you what we've already done."

Mary Nelle crossed her arms and shook her head, mumbling something I couldn't understand.

He waited for everyone to take a seat, then walked to the wall adjacent to the door and pointed to a large map of the park. "Let me review the search process. Day one, we started from the point where Morgan was last seen. Two rangers were placed on each trail leading out from that location. The next day a dog and trainer worked each trail. Some of the dogs were bloodhounds, who detect scents from the ground, and some were air scents dogs...Border Collies and German Shepherds. The next phase included off-trail searches, close to the point where the bandana was found." Shannon lightly placed his finger on the map. "We started in area 49, close to Cabin Flats Trail. We found the bandana approximately two hundred yard northeast of the Flats location. We made sweeps to Hughes Ridge, back north to Grassy Branch Trail, west toward Ice Water Spring, south to Kephart Prong Trail, and back to area 49."

"Why are you telling us this... to reinforce your failures?" I interrupted. "I don't need you rehashing attempts to find my wife. I need results not excuses."

Shannon steepled his fingers. "Earl, we've done everything humanly possible. Day after day, helicopters have surveyed the entire area for any signs of human activity. Nothing was found except the bandana. That's why we had to call off the search. But what Holvachek said is important. Fliers have been placed at every trail in this area. Hikers will notify us if they find evidence. They're a special breed. Their bond is tight, and they look after each other." He looked around the room, every word precise, trying to gain control. "Don't give up hope."

Hope. There was that empty word again. I turned, looked at Tony, then back at Melody. Not one face held the slightest glimmer of it.

Melody got up and walked toward Shannon as if each step was more difficult than the last. I'd never forget the *swoosh, swoosh, swoosh* of her leather soles on the faded brown carpet. She put her arms around Shannon's neck. "Please Mr. Shannon," she mumbled, "don't give up on my baby." Her body shook with sobs. "She's out there....I know she is. Don't give up, please." Her sobs became deeper and heavier and directly from her heart.

Shannon wrapped his arms around Melody's shoulders. "I'm so sorry...so sorry," he whispered.

I eased her away from him and pulled her to my chest. This had been a hard morning for everyone. These past days were too much — losing Morgan, losing hope, losing my mind.

After everyone filed out, Shannon stopped me at the door. "Earl —"

"I can't listen to you say you're sorry anymore." I could feel my earlier frustration simmering all over again. I pushed past him.

"I ran a background check on you and have the results."

I stopped halfway through the door and turned back around. Here it was. Shannon was going to give the report to the FBI, and they'd spend all their time investigating me instead of looking for whoever really took Morgan.

"The bar fights were in the past," he said. "I've seen your anguish over losing Morgan. You didn't have anything to do with it. That's what I told the FBI."

I stood still, almost afraid to breathe.

"Earl, you're not a person of interest in this case." He set his hand on my arm. "Do you hear what I'm saying?"

I nodded.

"Good." He nodded back and walked through the door, his shoulders drooped like giving up this search had cost him something too.

I went back to the condo both relieved that the FBI would concentrate on finding the real person who'd abducted Morgan and devastated that Shannon's earlier hunch had been right about the bandana being a way to throw off the search.

Melody and my family were going home. The thought of my trip back to New Jersey tomorrow without Morgan clawed at me like an army of ticked-off ants. I turned the television on hoping for some background noise to drown out my thoughts. A news story about the kidnapping flashed across the screen. My chest knotted tighter than a newborn's fist.

When Morgan's picture appeared on the screen, I ran my fingers over her image. "All I want to do is touch you.

Just a touch." Her innocent smile, long brown curls, and steel-blue eyes beckoned me, but all I could do was stare.

I went to the bathroom sink. My hands shook as I splashed cold water on my face. The mirror exposed a deep hollow circling my eyes. I hated my reflection. I hated myself. What kind of man can't protect his wife?

After drying my face, I stepped outside. Summer would soon give way to fall. The birds chirped like their song had been choreographed. Every sound, every whiff of a flower, everything reminded me of Morgan. Where was she?

A cool breeze swirled around my face. I took a deep breath and exhaled. Suddenly, I felt close to her. I didn't know why or how, but I wanted to think that maybe she was telling me she was okay.

CHAPTER 21

I'D BEEN HOME FROM TENNESSEE FIVE DAYS. I DIDN'T WANT TO see anyone. Didn't want to talk to anyone. The only company I wanted came in a bottle. How could I face my family? Or the community? What would they think? Kaura Brady, Morgan's best friend, probably hated me.

I was scraping the bottom of the ocean right now with no way to surface. I didn't know myself anymore. I'd crossed into a dark void. A void I feared would rip my heart out and leave me without a soul.

As I stepped out of my car in front of The Last Man Standing — a bar located smack dab in the bowels of Newark — the stench of urine off the hot pavement filled my nose. Neon beer lights on the building hissed and flashed on and off. The cracked, uneven sidewalk looked like a war zone in a third-world country.

Inside, I was greeted with a cloud of Mary Jane smoke. Customers filled folding chairs scattered around 1950s Formica tables. A string of multi-colored Christmas lights sagged loosely over the mirror behind the bar. Dante's Inferno couldn't look worse.

Stopping only to buy a bottle of whiskey at the bar, I moved straight to the back of the room and drank without a glass. A little while later, I glanced with double-vision at my watch. Eight o'clock. That couldn't be. No way had I been in this place for six hours.

The whiskey disagreed. Too much of it was gone.

I looked up. Two men were heading toward me. I blinked twice, trying to focus. "Tony, sit down and have a drink." I reached for the whiskey but couldn't find anything to pour it in. "Oops. Sorry, bid brubber." I pointed with a bent index finger. "Hey…it's Jim Pepper… Pepper…Jim Pepperman's standing right nessed to you, Tony."

Tony rested both hands on the table and leaned in. "It's time to go." He wasn't asking. He was telling.

I didn't like it. "No. Ain't ready. You can't tell me what to do. Buzz off." I motioned to him with the bottle, and it almost slipped out of my hand.

"Come on, little brother." He set his hand on my shoulder. "Let's go home."

"Get away from me." I swatted his hand. "You ain't my daaad."

Tony grabbed my shirt and pulled me over the table. One wooden table leg snapped like a dried twig and sent me sprawling on the dirty, concrete floor. The bottle crashed, and shards of glass splintered in a starburst pattern.

A crowd gathered in a semi-circle around us. Someone screamed, "Leave the guy alone." Another said, "You ain't leavin' here without gettin' busted up."

Jim faced the fever-pitched hecklers. "We didn't come here looking for trouble. This man's our brother. All we want to do is take him home. If one of you wants to stop us, step forward."

A big man, wearing gold chains around his neck and rings on every finger like Mr. T., looked like he might take Jim up on that.

Jim moved directly in front of him. "You want to try your luck on this honkie, tough guy?"

I still sat on the floor, having trouble focusing.

Mr. T rolled a toothpick around his large mouth and lunged at Jim.

A straight right cross caught the guy square on the chin. He went down like a bull on a frozen lake. Out cold.

I chuckled. That dude didn't know who he was messing with. Jim Pepperman was tougher than a leather boot and meaner than a pit bull.

Jim stepped over Mr. Gold Chains. "Anyone else want a piece of me?" His shout was so loud it rattled the smoke-stained windows.

The bunch of losers parted like a large-toothed comb on a mop of wet hair.

Jim got on one side of me, Tony the other, and walked me to the car.

I fell into the back seat. "Morgan, what have I done," I mumbled.

CHAPTER 22

JIM AND TONY JAMMED ME INTO THE BACKSEAT OF MY CAR outside the bar. My head bounced off the door frame like a bobblehead.

Tony pried the car keys out of my hand and gave them to Jim. He had to clear the front seat of empty beer cans, burger wrappers, and tricked out lottery tickets just to get in. My car—a dumpster on wheels.

A lighted billboard of the New York Yankees caught my attention. "Take me out to the ball park, take me out to the park, buy me some hot dogs and sauerkraut, I don't care if I ever get home. I love to sing when I'm drunk."

Jim reached back and shook my leg. "If you're going to sing, at least learn the right words."

"Okay…you funny, Jim."

When we pulled up to my house in Belleville, rain machine-gunned off the car. I opened my eyes to an electrical storm. Bony fingers of lightning flickered across the sky, temporarily blinding me.

Tony opened the car door and shook me. "Earl. Earl. Let's go buddy."

Jim assisted in pulling me out of the back seat—none too gentle—the big jerk.

A downpour slammed me against the car, but I managed to keep my balance even though my legs felt like two sticks of string cheese tied to my hips.

Tony moved his arm around my waist, and Jim placed my arm around his neck and shoulders. Somehow, with both of them grunting and groaning, we made it up the steps onto the porch where the roof sheltered us.

They dropped me into a vinyl, duct-taped chair.

"Hey." Tony tapped my cheek. "The house key?"

I wobble-waved my arm toward the door mat. "Under...there?"

My brother shook his head. "Gee, no one would ever think to look there."

Jim placed one hand on my head, gave a gentle twist, before laughing, maybe ribbing me about my trashed-out condition. His deep bass voice echoed in my aching, liquor-soaked brain.

My eyelids felt heavier than a sledgehammer. Correction, seven sledgehammers. And I let them fall. "I think I'm about to pass out."

Someone shook my shoulders and patted my cheeks.

"Get up, Earl," Tony yelled. "It's wet and cold." The sharpness in his voice signaled the babysitting had turned south.

My string-cheese legs supported me long enough to stumble inside and flip on the living room light before I nose-dived into the couch.

In another room, glass shattered on the floor.

"Jim, someone's in the kitchen." Tony whispered.

My heart didn't leap inside my chest. It ran out the front door.

Lightning crackled and flashed, followed by sonic-boom thunder. The overhead lights flickered but stayed on.

Two Tony's picked up an empty beer bottle, drew it back, and angled toward the kitchen. "Who's in there?" they called. "You'd better come out."

His all-business voice had me trying to stand, as if I'd be any help.

Tony soft-stepped to the kitchen wall, reached around the door frame, and turned on the light.

High-pitched screams spiked the air. Two cats shot off the kitchen table, onto the counter, and out the open window over the sink, sobering me faster than a pot of coffee.

Tony raked an empty carton of Pop's Tasty Wings off the counter and put down the beer bottle. "It seems the cats have been dining on your leftovers."

We caught our breath and sat in the living room. The house was a microcosm of my car. Dried pieces of half-eaten pepperoni lay on top of pizza boxes. The wedges looked like broken bits of pottery. French fries wormed inside Styrofoam containers with pools of ketchup smeared on the floppy lids. Empty beer bottles were stacked on the coffee table like bowling pins. The smell of rotting Chinese food could have the house condemned.

I looked down on my white T-shirt. A painter's pallet of everything I'd eaten today. And some of what I'd drunk. I tried to wipe off the stains. I was sorry Tony and Jim had to see me in this condition. When I looked at Tony there was only one of him now, but my vision was still fuzzy, his image blurring like an unfocused lens of a camera. He sat on the edge of the sofa, shoulders sagging.

"We need to get Earl dried out." Jim stood in the middle of the room. "Let's get him into the shower and in bed," he said to Tony. "I'll stay with him through Saturday. That's the first step. What do you think?"

Tony wiped a shaking hand over his mouth. "It's a start. If we need help, I know some counselors in Newark."

I glared at them and spat on the floor. Their plan to sober me up meant nothing to me. I had a plan too. An entirely different plan. And they couldn't stop it.

CHAPTER 23

Sunlight burst through a crack in my bedroom curtains in needle-sharp rays. Blinking hurt my swollen eyes. My head ached like someone had pounded me with a ball-peen hammer. I turned over. Slowly.

Tony and Jim were to blame. When they airmailed me into the backseat last night, my head had struck the roof of the car. I rubbed the robin's-egg knot on my head. Why had it seemed funny then?

Talking came from the living room. Had to be the TV. I picked up the alarm clock and tried to focus, but the numbers flashed faster than a roulette wheel. I blinked once, twice, and the wheel landed on 12:00 o'clock. Or something like that.

What happened last night? I remembered Tony and Jim pulling me out of the car like a piece of used furniture and cats meowing to high hell. Beyond that? God only knew.

I swung my legs to the side of the bed. Too fast. The hammer assaulting my head turned into a battering ram. My heartbeat pulsed in my eardrum. *Ka-boom. Ka-boom. Ka-boom.*

I swallowed, but my salivary glands didn't work. The inside of my mouth was as spiny and parched as a cactus.

Water. I needed water.

Pushing off the bed and aiming my body toward the kitchen took all my balancing skills. Hand-walking the walls kept me upright.

The kitchen sink was an oasis. I turned on the cold water, stuck my head under, and drank, drank, drank. I came up for air, then dove back into the cool, crisp water.

Out of the corner of my eye I caught a glimpse of Jim leaning against the door frame. He wore the same grin he always wore—the kind of grin that made me feel good. He'd never been judgmental, and I hoped he wouldn't be today.

"How about some ice water in a cup?" He walked to the cupboard, opened the door, and pulled out one of the two remaining clean glasses. Or mostly clean anyway.

My strength, sapped by days lost inside a drunken stupor, failed me. All I did was nod.

He opened the freezer. I stepped closer. A cold blast of air rushed over my face. I wanted to fold my body inside, shut the door, and fade into the numb reality of nothingness. Hypothermia was a painless way to go, right?

Jim pulled out a tray of ice and plopped cubes into the glass. Then he filled it with water and handed it to me.

Gulp. Gulp. Gulp. I finished off three glasses in a gnat's heartbeat.

Jim took the glass from me with his beefy paw. His hand reminded me of a catcher's mitt. "Feel better?"

Still too hung over to carry on a full conversation, I closed my eyes and nodded again.

With an arm around my back, he guided me to the living room couch. "Go ahead and lie down."

He didn't need to tell me to rest. The half-gallon of water I'd just inhaled had climbed up a ladder in my throat and was threatening to make a fire-hose exit. After settling on the sofa, I realized how stupid I'd been. The drinking binge had gone on for a week. The whiskey and beer hadn't solved any of my problems—not one. In fact, when I sobered up, I fully expected to find it had only added more. "What are you doing here?" I looked at Jim from the couch.

"Tony called. He thought you might listen to me."

I had a good idea of what he was going to say, and I wanted no part of any "rah-rah, we can get you through this mess" pep talk.

Jim pulled up a chair and started to place his size thirteens on the coffee table, but he didn't get the chair close enough. His heels barely nicked the table, and his shoes shot off like they'd been tied to a diesel truck. The expression on his face was monumental. He scratched his head, got out of his chair, pulled the table closer, sat down and eased his feet onto it.

I bit my cheeks to keep from laughing. Jim had something to say. I didn't want to ruin his tough-love moment.

"Here's how I see your situation," Jim said. "No one knows what you're going through, but I do know where you're headed. You can't avoid reality by drowning yourself in sorrow and rotten whiskey. One of two things is going to happen... Morgan's going to be found alive and you two can put your lives back together, or you're not going to see her again. But she'd want you to go on with your life, not destroy it. How you choose to handle the problem is up to you."

Who did he think he was—a super psychiatrist? He needed to get off my back and leave me alone. I knew what was best for me. I squared myself on the couch, feet on the floor. "First, I've got to ditch the booze. The heavy drinking only made things worse. Second, I need help, professional help. With my family, and that includes you, and counseling, I think I can beat this." I said everything he wanted to hear.

Jim leaped out of the chair. "That's the ticket. It's cliché, but I'm saying it anyway. The first step in solving a problem is to realize you have one."

He reached out his hand. A man hug followed.

I had to be alone. Everything was avalanching on me. My own guilt suffocated me. "Thanks for staying last night, but I need some time to clean this puke hole."

He pushed up his sleeves. "I'm good with helping."

"No, I'll do it. I'm embarrassed enough as it is. I'll call Tony and Mamma to let them know I'm okay. Oh, in case I forget, ask her if she'll make a meatloaf for dinner. I'll be there around six. You go see your mother."

Jim gave me another hug.

My living room had seen more hugs in the last hour than a two-day Helmsly family reunion.

"Okay," he said. "I had a feeling you had the guts to work through your problems. I'm proud. Proud indeed."

I nodded. If only he knew.

After Jim left, I sniffed my stale shirt and shuffled across the living room to the bathroom. I stepped into the shower, hoping it would wash away more than my stench. I needed it to wash away my guilt. Why had I left Morgan alone at the campsite? I should've stayed. Or cooked breakfast and then taken her to the falls. There were so many times I could've made different choices. Better choices. Safer choices.

Cold water stung my head like tiny electrical shocks, but nothing changed inside me. The only thing the water did was sober me enough to want to deal with the mess I'd made of the house. I didn't want anyone else to see it like that.

Drying off was a chore. My body shook like a naked man in a snow storm. I dressed with the skill of a three-year-old. Resting on the unmade bed, I tried to focus. Pain stabbed at the back of my head like a cattle prod. I pressed a hand over my eyes.

Because of the alcohol, I'd shamed my name, shamed myself, but most importantly, I'd shamed my family. Would I get forgiveness?

When the worst of the pain stopped, I looked around the bedroom. It was the least disgusting part of the house so I decided to start cleaning there. I didn't get far. A picture of Morgan on the chest of drawers stopped me, punching my heart where it was already bruised.

I picked up the photo. Morgan. Her blue eyes melted me every time I looked into them. What if I never saw that face again? Or felt her soft skin? Or heard the giggle that turned me inside out with happiness? Regret drowned me in a pool of emptiness. I turned the frame face down.

I made the bed first. Mamma always said if the bed was made, it made cleaning the rest of the house easier. I tackled the dirty clothes scattered across the room next. Two or three armloads shoved into the closet solved my problem. What you couldn't see wasn't there.

The kitchen and living room were the worst. A mix of a garbage dump and a fraternity bash gone wrong, it took two hours to clean. And still only looked half-decent. A filthy house was the flip side of Morgan. When I finished, ten large garbage bags jammed the trash cans in the alley.

CHAPTER 24

AFTER I CLEANED THE HOUSE, I DROVE TO THE PARK ACROSS the street from Mamma's. I got out and crossed the playground to a picnic table in front of her house. Waist-high shrubs concealed me.

The tall oak trees shaded her gray wood-framed home with white-trimmed windows. The dark green grass was perfectly manicured on this warm September day. Red and yellow roses nestled around the long front porch creating a perfect Norman Rockwell painting, but inside the all-American house, Mamma worried over me. She knew I wasn't coping well over Morgan's kidnapping.

I'd been at the picnic table ten minutes when Tony pulled into the driveway, got out, and opened the gate of the white picket fence.

Mamma stepped out of the house waving both arms like a pinwheel at a circus booth. "Where's Jim? I want to know about Earl. Why ain't he with you?" When Mamma got nervous, her voice pitched high.

Tony shook his head and chuckled. He wrapped his arms around her weight-lifter shoulders and hugged her.

"Dat Jim is always late except when it comes to eatin.'" She put both hands on Tony's shoulder and pushed.

I knew she loved Jim as much as her own. She made a fist and tapped, tapped Tony's nose in a playful gesture.

She stepped around him, swatted his rump, and went inside. It looked as though Tony's calmness rubbed off on her.

Tony sat on the porch swing, one hand high up on the support chains. His slow, deliberate push moved the swing back and forth, back and forth, back and forth. After Mamma left, his smile disappeared, and he seemed to stare off into space.

Was he thinking about me? Was I making everyone's life miserable? I hated myself.

A few minutes later Jim pulled up in front of the house.

I couldn't stand it anymore. I got off the picnic table and walked back to my car. I had unfinished business.

Back at the house, I set Morgan's picture and my SEAL trident pin on the table next to the recliner in the living room. I sat and cushioned both arms on the chair. My heels tapped the floor.

"Morgan." I breathed her name like a tribute. "These past few weeks you've been on my mind constantly. It's as though I've known you all my life...at the same time, it's like we just met. I never thought I could love someone as much as I love you. Driving down to the wedding, I imagined us being married fifty years, our children grown, and us on the back porch watching a summer rain."

I slid my wedding ring off and on. "Today...I wish I'd never met you. You'd still be alive. I'm so...so sorry. I love you, Morgan. You brought life to me I'd never experienced."

I stared at her picture. A different kind of fear gripped me — a fear that ravaged my spirit with crushing talons. I gasped for air. I wanted to get up and run, start over, but how? The invisible beast pushed me back into the chair, forcing me to endure the guilt of my mistakes. There was nowhere to run. I had to face the guilt head on.

From behind my back, I pulled my service pistol from the holster, chambered a round, slacked the trigger, and placed the gun to my temple.

CHAPTER 25

WHEN I LEANED BACK, THE RECLINER CREAKED. I GRIPPED THE pistol pointed at my temple. My hand shook.

Knock. Knock. A sharp rap on the door interrupted my solitude.

"What the...?" My teeth clenched so hard, my cheek muscles quivered.

Knock. Knock.

I laid the pistol on the table next to the recliner, walked to the door, and looked through the peephole.

A large man, big-brother-Tony large, but younger, knocked again. A black chauffeur's hat pulled down tight over his head. Muscles crammed his black suit, and his white button-down shirt stretched tight around his bulldog neck. The dark sunglasses reminded me of a secret service agent.

I opened the door.

"You Earl Helmsly?" His deep voice sounded threatening.

I closed the door halfway, but I couldn't reach the pistol if he forced the issue. "Who are you, and what do you want?"

"Are. You. Earl. Helmsly?" This time he sounded irritated.

I took a deep breath and stared at my reflection in his dark shades. "Yes."

He handed me a big manila envelope.

I took it from him.

"Read what's inside." He turned and started toward the long, black manicured limousine.

I looked at the sealed envelope. "Who you are?" I slammed the door behind me and followed him.

He whipped around. "Stop." His large mouth exposed rows of chalky, white teeth, and he pointed at me with his index finger. "Don't come any closer. Do. You. Understand?" His words bounced off my chest.

I nodded.

He walked to the driver's side door, got in, and drove off.

The windows were too dark to see inside.

I walked back into the house. The envelope was bulky and soft. I pinched the metal clasps together, folded the flap back, reached inside, and pulled out a black ski mask. I laid the mask on the couch and removed a typed letter.

Mr. Helmsly,

We may have information about the whereabouts of your wife, Morgan. Be at the empty warehouse near the Brooklyn Bridge at 66 Frank Street tonight at 10:00 o'clock. Pull down the alley and park at the back of the building. Bring nothing with you. Tell no one. There will be other cars. Do not get out until the light over the door is turned off then back on. Put on the ski mask and come inside. Others will follow. Do not

*speak to anyone. And I repeat, tell no one, and bring
no one. If you do, there will be consequences.*

The letter slipped from my hands and drifted to
the floor.

CHAPTER 26

I PICKED UP THE LETTER. THE PRINT BLURRED. THE RECLINER behind me caught my falling body. The trembling in my fingers moved into my chest and messed with my breathing until it became short, panting gasps. My vision scrambled the words, confusing like the letters of a scrabble game.

I read the letter again. Morgan. Alive. A sick joke or a flicker of possibility? Moments ago I'd held a gun to my head, ready to give up. I looked at the pistol on the side table, then closed my eyes.

What-if's peppered me like a machine gun. Not about the past and what I'd done wrong, but about the future. What if Morgan *was* still alive, and I'd pulled that trigger? What if I'd been in a bar when the limousine came by? What if I'd ignored the knock?

I picked up the gun, took it to the bedroom, and locked it in the gun safe. If I didn't find Morgan, it'd be waiting for me.

Ring. Ring. Ring.

I reached to answer the call, then changed my mind. It might be Tony or Mamma. The note said tell no one. I had to get out of here. My car keys. Where were they? I patted my pockets. Not there. The drawer next to the bed. Yes. I grabbed them, stopping to get the ski mask and letter. Fumbling with the key, I got in the car, and sped out of the driveway.

I had no idea where 66 Frank Street was in Brooklyn, but I knew the general location of the old warehouse district. That part of New York hadn't been used in years. The only inhabitants were empty whiskey bottles, the occasional dirty blanket, and people society had turned their backs on.

The drive took an hour. The closer I got, the more hope spiked inside me until I was quietly whispering, "Morgan, Morgan, Morgan."

A rusty, lopsided, green-and-white street sign marked Frank Street. I eased down the road, glancing back and forth at the buildings, my heart thumping against my ribs. Building 66 came up quickly on my right. I jammed on the brakes.

The rows of blacked-out windows framed by stained and chipped red bricks and concrete loading docks with dented metal doors painted a picture of gangsters hiding their liquor barrels during prohibition.

I wiped a hand across my dry mouth and took a deep breath. Pulling forward, I saw the alley leading to the back of the building. Should I go down now? Not a good idea. If someone saw me, it might draw unwanted attention.

Seven o'clock. Three hours to kill. No food all day. Enough time to eat. Too much time to wait.

CHAPTER 27

Driving around the streets of New York annoyed me. The traffic noise never stopped — the swoosh of screaming tires as they turned the corners, the clank of cars passing over manhole covers, the heavy breaths of bus engines idling.

I glanced at my watch — 9:05. Better head to the warehouse. I couldn't afford to get hung up in traffic. Yeah. Right. A measly five blocks away, at most, and there was less traffic than Belleville's Main Street on Saturday night. I needed to settle down.

Frank Street. Just ahead on the right. As the hands on my watch moved to 9:30, I pulled over and parked. Too early to show up at the warehouse.

The wind picked up. Newspapers skipped over the hood of the car and wrapped around a light pole. I looked at the rundown building and shivered. A flash of lightning burst white in the night sky over the city. As if I wasn't anxious enough.

I looked at my watch again. 9:45. I started the car, turned on the lights, and pulled away from the curb. Frank Street. I slowed and made the turn, hoping I could see the faded number on the warehouse. There it was — 66.

I turned down the alley and parked at the back entrance. A gust of wind slammed into the side of the car. Air whistled through my partially opened window like an omen warning me something evil lurked inside the building.

My stomach tightened. What the heck was I doing? This could be a trap set by the same people who kidnapped Morgan. I sucked in a deep breath and slowly exhaled. But what if it wasn't? What if it was legit? Even if there was a one-percent chance of finding Morgan, I had to take it.

The light over the metal door glowed like a beacon for ships at sea on a moonless night. 9:58. Two cars pulled in behind me, then three more. Maybe this *was* legit.

My heart rate tripled. 9:59. I reached for my ski mask. It wasn't on the seat where I thought I put it. I scrapped the trash onto the floorboard and ran my hand between the seat and the back rest. Not there. I glanced at the door.

The light went off, then back on. Where was the mask? A rush of nerves started at my toes and raced through my body to my brain.

Others were getting out of their cars.

No, no, no. Where. Was. The. Mask? I felt on the floorboard between my legs. Nothing. I ran my hand over the dashboard. Yes. I grabbed it and jerked it on. I got out of the car, my knees wobbling like an old man.

Just as I reached the warehouse, the door swung open. The chauffeur who delivered the letter stepped out, shut it behind him, looked at us like he had the strength to reach in and yank our throats out. "Inside there is a circle of chairs. Take a seat. Do not talk." He didn't have to repeat it. There was something about his robotic tone that made me pay attention.

He reached back without looking and opened the door.

I was the last to enter.

A large flood light beamed down from the ceiling. It reminded me of an interrogation tactic used by SEALS in prisoner survival training. Whoever set this up probably had a military background. Six chairs formed a circle at least eight feet in diameter. All of us sat. The masks hid our faces, but we could see each other's eyes.

Minutes went by.

Nothing happened.

Sweat gathered around the eyelids of my mask. The hood itched. Too hot. Too tight. It took all my willpower to keep from yanking it off.

More minutes passed.

The sound of a tugboat horn echoed in the distance. Lightning crackled. Thunder rattled the dark, painted windows. Wind punched metal loading dock doors. Battle images raced through my mind slide-show style. I loved challenges — facing the unknown — but hated the consequences that often followed.

The high-pitched screech of a bad speaker system snapped my thoughts to attention. "Gentlemen, all of you received a letter that brought you here tonight." The altered voice of the person talking added to the creepiness. "My daughter was abducted and is being held in a remote area around Gatlinburg, Tennessee. I'm looking to put together a rescue mission."

Abducted. A rescue mission. A chance to bring Morgan home. It was real. Morgan hadn't wandered off. Hadn't got lost. Hadn't run away. She'd been *taken*. Images of someone hurting her stabbed me in the gut.

I looked around the circle at the way the other men held themselves, at their builds, at the seriousness in their eyes. I'd bet my last breath everyone in the circle had special-ops training. It just made sense.

The speaker crackled again. "Several women are being held with her." There was a long pause and then, "One of you has a special interest in the mission. His wife went missing while camping in The Smoky Mountains. I have reason to believe you'll find her with my daughter."

My head dropped. My eyes grew cloudy.

"Twenty-five thousand dollars will be paid to each of you to get these women back. Should you choose not to participate, leave now with your mask on. You have five minutes to decide."

No one left.

CHAPTER 28

IN THE CIRCLE UNDER THE LIGHT, EACH MAN PEELED OFF HIS ski mask. I folded mine on my lap. Eager to talk first, I shifted in my seat. "I'm Earl Helmsly, former Navy Seal. My wife's been abducted."

The silence was almost reverent as the other men nodded. Tension lurked in front of us like a ten-foot brick wall. How would we push through the barrier to build a cohesive unit? All the men looked physically fit. But, mentally, would they be up for the challenge? Was the reward money their only motivation? Could I trust them?

"I'm Stan Kowalski, retired Delta Force." The guy directly across from me, square-jawed and bull-necked, had short salt-and-pepper hair cut high and tight. Narrow light-blue eyes added to his quiet, but imposing presence. "What's your wife's name?" His powerful voice elevated my confidence.

"Morgan." Out of respect for her, I straightened in my chair. I knew nothing about this man, but I got the feeling he'd walk through hell and yank Morgan out of the devil's hand if he had the chance. If I had to bet, I'd say Kowalski was a no nonsense, no BS warrior who lived by a code of justice.

The guy next to him scratched his head, his long black hair slick with perspiration. His beefy legs didn't seem to match his average upper body. "I'm Cajun. Manley Pharts. Ya spell it P-H-A-R-T-S. Dat's right. Pharts." He laughed, his shoulders bouncing up and down, along with his slicked-back locks. When he finally stopped, his grin exposed a huge gap between his two front teeth. "Marine Recon."

Everyone looked at each other and laughed so loud it echoed in the empty building. He had to be the class clown of the group. I was grateful he broke the tension.

The man to my right said, "Pharts. I love it." His back flush to the chair, he rested his hands on his thighs. "Joe Valenzuela. Army Ranger." Coal black hair matched his dark, viper-like eyes. He stretched out a pair of the biggest boots I'd ever seen.

The man directly to my left reached into his back pocket and pulled out a pouch of Red Man tobacco and stuffed a fistful into his mouth.

He didn't look like the chewing type. Not with his short, curly black hair and a baby face that didn't jive with the mountains of muscles pushing against his shirt. The guy had to be in the neighborhood of two-fifty. And I had no doubt, if he stood, he'd tower over me. I'd put him at 6'4" minimum.

"Andy Zorbas." After several chomps he muttered, "Army Ranger." He gave Valenzuela an index finger salute. Brothers in arms.

The last person in the circle was a slight young man, definitely the smallest of the team. His wavy red hair, quick smile, and wire-framed glasses reminded me of a Catholic priest from an old movie. "I'm Shane Cassity.

Irish Defense Force." If he hadn't added in that last part, his brogue and lightly-freckled complexion would have outed him as an Irishman.

Strange how no one knew the guy next to him, but a bond seemed to be working its way around the circle. My earlier hunch had been right on—all these men had special ops backgrounds.

The door of the warehouse opened, letting in the street light. The chauffeur approached the group with heavy steps that smacked the concrete floor. He clasped his hands behind his back. "Gentlemen, please park your vehicles in this building. I'll take you to a private airport, and from there you'll leave for Tennessee."

"Who's putting this together, and when will we meet him?" I stood. My questions couldn't wait any longer.

"In due time." The driver cranked a stern look my way and buttoned his tailored black jacket. "He'll be on the plane with you. Please, we must go now."

After the vehicles were parked in the warehouse, the group was especially quiet. I suppose, like every mission, each man dealt with the unknown in different ways. But one thing was certain, considering the backgrounds of all these men, the undertaking would be dangerous. The only difference for me were the stakes—Morgan's life and my sanity.

A long, black van pulled inside the building. We lined up, waiting our turn to get inside in complete silence. Silence so familiar I swore I was back in the Navy on deployment day.

The van, jam-packed with large bodies, heated up quickly. Sweat broke out on my upper lip.

"I think I'll call you Jupiter, King of the Gods." Pharts sat next to Zorbas.

"Why would you do that?" Zorbas looked straight ahead, stiff as a mannequin in Macy's front window.

"Zorbas, ain't that a Greek name?" Pharts asked.

The roar of an eighteen-wheeler going past us in the opposite direction muffled his question.

"Yes." Zorbas chomped down on his chaw of tobacco, and his jaw popped.

"So you're strong like a king of the mystical gods. The name just fits." Pharts continued.

"Mythical, not mystical."

"What?" Pharts' tone lifted like he was annoyed.

"You mean mythical gods. Not mystical."

"Whatever...I'm still calling you Jupiter."

"No, you're not." Zorbas chuckled, loosening up a bit.

"Why not?" Pharts' tone spiked.

I heard a soft chuckle behind me.

"Jupiter is a Roman god, not a Greek god." Cassity joined the conversation.

Pharts took a deep breath and snorted like a racehorse.

Another chuckle, this one a little louder, came from a man in front of me. The other men were obviously enjoying the conversation.

"Fine, what's the name of the king of the Greek gods?" Pharts asked. His tone seemed bored and fed up with all the dialogue.

"Zeus."

Pharts' arms went straight up. "Even better. Zeus starts with Z just like Zorbas. Hot damn." His loud voice mixed with a hint of sarcasm.

Everyone laughed. Pharts was going to keep us sane. Good for him.

I tuned out the conversation, my thoughts turning to Morgan. The van windows were shaded, and I couldn't read the street signs. It took thirty minutes to get to the private airport. We pulled past a hanger, and the van stopped short of the nose of a Boeing 757 parked on the runway.

As we piled out, I noticed Zorbas still chewing on the tobacco he had back at the warehouse. I hadn't noticed where he'd been spitting. I tapped him on the shoulder. "Zeus, where's the bottle?"

"What bottle?

"You have to spit somewhere. Where's the bottle?"

"Who says I have to spit?"

"You mean you don't spit?"

He rolled the wad from one cheek to the other and shook his head. "Nope." The guy had to be tougher than the backend of a water buffalo.

I followed him up the steps of the plane into the seating area. The cabin reminded me of a five-star hotel. A lounge area with an L-shaped couch and a large television was in the middle of the plane surrounded by mahogany tables and sleek cream recliners finished with gold seat buckles. The galley, with rich wood-grained cabinets, didn't look like any kitchen I'd been in. The door to the bathroom was open. The marble sinks came with gold faucets. At the back of the plane, an open door exposed a queen-size bed.

Luxurious didn't begin to describe the magnificent aircraft. Who put this group together? How rich was he? How did he know about Morgan? More importantly, why did he care?

CHAPTER 29

GAWKING LIKE A BUNCH OF SCHOOL KIDS, THE GUYS HAWK-eyed the plane, me included.

"Please take a seat and buckle up." A crackled voice came over the intercom. "Prepare for takeoff."

I took a recliner next to the L-shaped sofa and strapped in. The chair molded to the shape of my body. The leather smelled fresh and clean, like the interior of a new car, with a hint of vanilla.

The other men found their spots. The pilot revved the engines. The plane taxied down the runway, the tips of its wings bouncing like an awkward gooney bird's first flight. Motors growled like some underworld beast, pushing the plane forward. Our speed picked up until the bumpy runway gave way to the soft, peaceful whisper of the jet engine.

Manhattan's skyline passed by my window. The bright lights, so beautiful and peaceful, masked a city shrouded in darkness and crime — the same evil that stole my Morgan.

Exhilaration lit a fire inside me. I hadn't felt like this in weeks. Morgan — she was all I could think about. And now there was a chance to get her back.

The mission sponsor didn't appear to be on the plane. Clearly, the chauffeur had lied.

I stiffened and dug my fingers into the leather chair arms. My heart sputtered, chest tightened. When a tribal chief had lied to our SEAL team, the mission had failed, and I'd lost brothers. Moving to the middle of the plane, I called the men together. "The chauffeur said the person funding this mission would be with us. He ain't here. Do you get the feeling we've been sold a bill of goods?"

Kowalski crisscrossed his hands. "Maybe the guy changed his mind and plans to meet us there. Let's not get ahead of ourselves and panic."

Pharts spoke. "I've got a pilot's license if we want to mutiny."

"What kind of license?" Skepticism dripped off each of Kowalski's words.

"Single engine. Prop driven." Pharts' chest popped out like he'd just been given the Medal of Honor.

"Do you really think you could land a 757?" Mr. Pharts would be sprawled on the deck with a Swiss-cheese chest if Kowalski's eyes had been fifty-caliber machine guns.

"Gentlemen, have a seat." The baritone voice came from a short, bald man leaning against the open cockpit door, arms folded. "My name is Max Hopson. I'm responsible for the mission. I own this plane. I'm the pilot. I assure you, I can land it."

He looked like Wilford Brimley. Morgan and I had seen him on a television special this summer.

Mr. Hopson wasn't tall, but by no means was he small. His broad shoulders, thick wrists, thick glasses, and thick mustache weren't what I pictured for a mogul, not even close, but his confident gait toward us indicated a man used to taking charge.

He pointed to the L-shaped couch for us to sit. "My co-pilot's a retired Air Force Colonel with twenty years of flight service, just in case you're wondering. Please have a seat and let me explain the reason for this mission."

All of us sat, giving Hopson our full attention.

"I own MH Enterprises, a world-wide corporation dealing in everything from oil products to weapons manufacturing for the government to toilet paper."

Most of us grinned at the toilet-paper comment.

Hopson walked to a cabinet on the wall and raised a roll-top door to reveal a whiteboard. With a blue marker, he wrote *DONA*. "Dona is my daughter." He pronounced it like Donna. "She was named after my father, Don. I hate it when people don't say her name correctly."

This guy not only looked like Wilford Brimley, he sounded like him too.

"Six weeks ago, Dona disappeared from the University of Tennessee campus after a night class. All leads went cold in Knoxville. The police found her car at an abandoned farm in Gatlinburg last week." He cleared his throat, swallowed, and pushed his glasses up on his nose. "To make a long story short, I hired a Cherokee whose family has lived in the Smoky Mountain for hundreds of years to scout the area. He found moonshine stills off the Appalachian Trail. He reconned the area for three days and two nights, reporting that multiple women were being held captive at the whiskey distilling site."

This *was* a real mission. And maybe a real chance to find Morgan.

Hopson adjusted his pants, his girth hanging over his belt. "I encouraged Dona to attend the University of Tennessee because people in the South aren't as familiar with the name Hopson as they are in the North. It's clear whoever has her has no idea what a prize they have, or I would be dealing with a ransom situation. I read in the Gatlinburg paper that Morgan Helmsly disappeared in this area. My scout said he saw a black woman at the camp. She could be your wife, Earl."

Thoughts circled my head like a Ferris wheel, rising and falling between exhilaration and despair. What if it wasn't Morgan? No. Couldn't think about that now. I leaned forward, closed my eyes, and thanked God for bringing Mr. Hopson into the picture. Tears gathered. I quickly flicked them away with my thumb.

Hopson looked at me, his gaze penetrating and focused. Those eyes were the eyes of someone used to getting what he came for. He took a step back, resting against the whiteboard. "I hand-picked you because of your skills. You're professionals. You've all had high success rates on rescue missions. I did not pick a leader. You're a team now, and that's for the team to decide."

We all looked at each other.

"Helmsly has the most wood in the fire." Kowalski spoke first. "I say he's team leader."

"I'm too close to this. When we find Morgan, she'll need me." I wrung my hands. "Someone else take charge."

"Who's been on the most missions?" Valenzuela questioned.

"Twelve for me," Kowalski said, "but not as command and control leader."

"How many were successful?" Cassity adjusted his wire-framed glasses, his brogue thick as Irish stew.

Kowalski stroked his five o'clock shadow and hesitated. "Twelve." Something flickered in his eyes.

Something I couldn't read. Why did he hesitate? Had he lost his nerve?

"How many casualties?" Cassity spoke again.

Kowalski slowly turned his head toward Cassity. "If you're asking about deaths, none." His tone was firm in a way that highlighted leadership.

Cassity's eyes flashed. "Good enough for me. I vote Kowalski to lead the charge."

Kowalski's eyes bore a hole into our souls as though he wanted a hundred percent approval before he accepted the team lead.

And no one said a word to the contrary.

Kowalski looked back at Hopson and nodded.

Hopson nodded back. "Let's do this."

Kowalski said, "Tell me what you know about the location."

"There are two sites about one-hundred-fifty yards apart," Hopson replied. "Both have stills and cabins. The women are split up and housed in the shacks."

"How many women?" Kowalski asked.

"Between five and six."

"How many moonshiners at the camp at night?"

"No more than four."

"How many during the day?"

"Twelve to fifteen."

Kowalski sucked in air and exhaled. "This is gonna cause a problem. Because of the close proximity of the two camps, the attacks will have to take place at night at the same time. We'll need special equipment. Will that be a problem?"

"I'm an arms manufacturer." Hopson chuckled. "Won't be an issue. I've gathered general supplies, but I don't have the military expertise to know specific items you'd prefer. That you'll have to tell me. But with the two camps split, I figured two snipers would be needed. I selected Zorbas and Valenzuela. Their marksmanship is top shelf."

"What kind of rifles?" Kowalski looked at Valenzuela and Zorbas.

"M-24 ADL with starlight scopes," Valenzuela replied. "That good for you, Zorbas?"

"Yup."

Kowalski walked to a table, pulled out a chair, and sat. He alternated finger taps as though he was thinking. He looked at Hopson. "Could the scout tell if the men at the site had any military training?"

Hopson moved to the table across from Kowalski. "I don't know. We'll have to get with my man in Tennessee. He was still putting reports together when I left to meet you in New York."

"If the moonshiners are ex-military, and if they were special ops, they'll set up countermeasures for protection, booby traps, that sort of thing." Kowalski's eyes focused at the center of the table.

Hopson leaned back in his chair, palms up, indicating he didn't know.

"Cassity, Pharts, and Earl, are you okay with M-16 rifles?" Kowalski was every bit the team leader I needed.

"Good to go," Pharts said in his slow, Cajun voice.

I nodded to Kowalski.

"The M-16 is my weapon of choice," Cassity said. "And my specialty is explosives, if you're interested."

Kowalski's eyes lit up like a kid in Baskin Robbins. "What explosives do you need?"

"A couple of hand grenades and some tripwire should do the trick."

Things were beginning to click. Someone needed to grab my arm to keep me from floating to the top of the plane. I had real hope about getting Morgan back alive.

A question mark stamped Kowalski's face. He stared at Hopson. "Hand grenades, is that possible?"

"Does a bird poop on mailboxes?"

Everyone laughed. The team seemed to be coming together.

"How are we going to communicate?" Zorbas beat me to the punch.

"We'll need FM-PRC-77 radios and stopwatches and military watches to sync our attacks. The guards will have to be taken out at the same time," Kowalski said.

"Better get us plenty of deer musk to hide our scents in case of dogs." Valenzuela brought up a good point.

"Hey," Pharts interrupted, "my stomach thinks my throat's been cut. When can we eat?"

Hopson pointed. "Food's in the galley. Help yourself."

"Mr. Hopson?" Kowalski broke in. "Where will the team be staying? We still have planning to do."

"A retreat area near Knoxville, not far from our landing strip."

My focus sharpened. The plane couldn't get to Tennessee fast enough. The poor SOBs who took my wife had no idea what they'd be dealing with, but they'd soon find out, and it wouldn't be pretty.

Hopson pushed back from the table and walked toward the front of the plane.

I'd always had butterflies before a mission. This one was no different. I closed my eyes. Morgan—I'm coming. Just hang on. I opened my eyes as Hopson reached the cockpit.

"One other thing," Kowalski called. "We'll be outnumbered after the night raid. Can you get me an M-60 machine gun?"

Hopson cocked his head to one side, pulled off his glasses, and tugged on his bushy eyebrow. "I'd think by now, you'd realize I can get you any doggone thing you want."

Kowalski smiled, amused. "Sorry I asked."

CHAPTER 30

THE MEN AND I RESTED ON THE PLANE AFTER OUR MEAL. Kowalski said he'd go over the Five Paragraph Operation Order when we landed. That was vital for the rescue to be successful.

We reached Tennessee just before the sun came up.

Hopson left the cockpit and walked to us. "There's a van waiting to take us to the hidden retreat. I've constructed mock-ups of the still and two cabins. You can have as many dry runs as you want until you feel comfortable with the rescue. Success is crucial."

I was impressed with Hopson. By the looks on the other men's faces, they were too.

The van took us to a large log structure in a remote location in the Smoky Mountains. No doubt Hopson's mansion. It was no hunting lodge. One tree remained in the center of the main room. The rest of the house was built around this feature. Massive trees were used to make the furniture. A spiral staircase led to the upstairs bedrooms. I saw five doors leading to those rooms. The logs had been stained with light-colored varnish. One wall was floor-to-ceiling glass. I'd never seen anything like it.

Hopson stood near the glass wall and pointed to a huge green tent on the back lawn. "Check the equipment, make sure you have the gear you need, and locate your weapon.

"How much ammo is each man allowed?" I directed the question to Kowalski.

"Enough for three days." Kowalski turned to Hopson. "Will that be a problem?" It was the second time he'd questioned Hopson's ability to produce the materials we needed.

Hopson stared at Kowalski

He caught Mr. Hopson's drift. "Never mind."

We all went into the tent. It was like a candy store for military personnel, filled with weapons, camo clothes, food rations, and everything else we'd asked for.

The snipers, Valenzuela and Zorbas, went to the M-24's, worked the bolt actions, and looked through the starlight scopes. Both men went to Kowalski. Valenzuela spoke. "We don't see the suppressors."

Kowalski looked back to Hopson, who was talking to Cassity. "You go tell him. I don't have the cojones."

Valenzuela flicked the end of his nose. A nervous twitch? "Kowalski, we can improvise. All we need to make the suppressors are empty Coke cans and steel wool."

Kowalski rubbed his stubbled face. "You good with improvising, Zorbas?"

"Done it lots of times." Zorbas grinned. "Not an issue."

Valenzuela nodded.

"So who's going to push for the steel wool?" Kowalski questioned.

"I'd rather ask for steel wool than watch Mr. Deep Pockets blow a gasket over not having the suppressors," Zorbas quipped.

Kowalski smiled and gave Zorbas a thumbs up. "Okay, make it work."

Zorbas gave Valenzuela a one-handed pat on the upper arm. "You ask him for the steel wool."

Valenzuela scrunched his shoulders. "Why me?"

Zorbas slid his lower jaw back and forth, probably thinking of a good answer. "Because your feet are bigger than mine."

I chuckled. Didn't see that coming.

"What?" Valenzuela scratched his left butt cheek.

Zorbas gave him a gentle nudge with both hands. "Go on, dude."

"What am I going to say?"

"You'll think of something."

The two slowly approached Mr. Hopson. I would've loved to be a bug on their shoulders to hear the conversation.

"What in billy goat's heaven do you need steel wool for?" Hopson bellowed.

Valenzuela's hand motions were nonstop for a full fifteen seconds. When he stopped moving, Hopson nodded. The two snipers turned and walked back toward me. They looked like kids who'd robbed the cookie jar and gotten away with it.

I couldn't wait to hear what he told the billionaire. "What did you tell him you needed the steel wool for?" I crossed my arms in front of my chest. This was gonna be good.

Valenzuela adjusted his belt, like he was proud. "I told him it was an Aztec warrior tradition to wipe with steel wool on your first dump of a mission, a sign of toughness and good luck."

I chuckled and shook my head. "Why didn't you just tell him the truth?"

"And miss the reaction on his face?" Valenzuela laughed so hard his body shook.

The guys were already special. The camaraderie couldn't be explained — why men would be willing to sacrifice their lives for total strangers. And money had little to do with it.

CHAPTER 31

AS THE SUN SET OVER THE SMOKY MOUNTAINS, I TOOK A SHORT walk through the tall birch trees to get a minute alone. A single crow squawked in a far-off valley, and the cool evening air pushed against the warmth of the day. At that moment, the world seemed peaceful.

Hopson said tonight we'd meet Phillip Blackhawk, the Cherokee who found the campsite and the moonshine stills. When we'd finished at the supply tent late that morning, Kowalski told us to have lunch and grab a couple of hours of rest before meeting tonight. He needed our bodies and minds fresh and alert.

My heart ached for Morgan, but the excitement of seeing her again overruled the torture I'd lived with the past few weeks. I wanted to believe the moonshiners had her, but I needed reassurance.

Darkness moved in reminding me I had to get back.

Something moved dead leaves in front of me.

I stiffened. My adrenalin spiked.

It happened again.

Someone or something had maneuvered behind me. I turned. "What the…?" My heart two-stepped across my chest.

A man stood not five feet from me.

I squared to meet him. "Who are you?" My tone and my posture were battle ready.

"Peace brother. I mean you no harm. I'm Phillip Blackhawk. Max Hopson hired me."

He was average height. His black flat-top, green T-shirt, jeans, and hunting boots didn't jive with my mental image of a Cherokee.

I wiped a backhand across my forehead. "You scared the life out of me. How long have you been there?"

"I followed you up the mountain, off to your left. When you sat, I worked my way behind you. I had to toss two rocks to get your attention."

I paused and stared at him. That didn't bode well for my reaction time. My SEAL instincts must be getting rusty.

"I'm not what you pictured, am I?" His words mixed with his laughter. "You expected me to be wearing a straight-rimmed black felt hat with a feather in the band, long braids, and a plaid shirt with a vest. Right?" His smile was warm and friendly.

"That's pretty close." I immediately liked him, and we shook hands.

As the sun dipped behind the trees, we walked down the mountain to the lodge. Halfway there, I grabbed Blackhawk's arm. "Can you describe the black lady at the still site?"

He paused, his head angled upward. "I've only seen her through a window, not much for me to describe, but she had long brown hair."

My knees wobbled, every tension-packed muscle relaxed. "Thank you." His minor description was all the reassurance I needed.

The hours couldn't pass fast enough.

After supper, we gathered in the large living room to go over the plan. Hopson brought in a whiteboard.

Kowalski wrote *Five Paragraph Operation Order* across the top, then the number one under that. "Paragraph One — the situation. Five or six women held hostage by a group of numbnuts at the distilling site. Dona, Mr. Hopson's daughter, has been confirmed as one of them, and Earl's wife is thought to be with her. Paragraph Two — our mission. To safely extract the hostages and capture as many mountain thugs as possible. Paragraph Three — the concepts of the operation. How will we, as a team, carry out the mission? What do we need to know?"

I raised my hand. "If there are two camps, how far apart are they? How many guards at night, and how will the team be divided?"

Kowalski pointed to Blackhawk. "Fill us in. Hopson briefly told us about the two sites."

Blackhawk walked to the front of the room. I hadn't noticed, but he was bow-legged and pigeon-toed. "The two camps are about two hundred yards apart around the mountain. At night, there are four guards, two at each site. The women are split up between the camps. One guard stays inside with the women. One man waits outside. Hopson passed on your concerns about the mountain men being ex-military. I saw no evidence of that kind of training, and I found no booby traps. One thing to your advantage, these men appear to be self-secured with their operation. They won't be expecting a raid."

Relief seemed to spread among the team. My confidence swelled knowing the mission didn't deal with people trained to hold a position. The surprise element would give us an edge.

Blackhawk continued. "Now the downside. The men carry automatic weapons, Russian made AK-47s, and all of them probably know every inch of these mountains. Withdrawing is going to be difficult. We'll have a fight on our hands."

I took another look at the men. All were stone-faced.

"Do you know the leader?" Zorbas asked.

Blackhawk grabbed a chair, twisted it, and sat with his chest facing the backrest. "The others call him Worm. He's tall and slender with blond hair spiked four or five inches. And his eyes, they're cold and sunken. One day he brought a wounded doe to camp and gutted the defenseless animal alive for supper."

The room went silent to the point where I heard the man next to me breathing.

"Payback." I broke the silence. "It's payback time."

The rescue had enough motivation, but this just added spice to the salsa. I was sick of feeling helpless. Sick of being controlled by fear. Sick of people doing terrible things to others. "Is Worm there day and night?"

"He was there every day," Blackhawk said, "but stayed only one night."

"Earl, you asked how the team would be divided," Kowalski broke in. "It's my opinion Valenzuela and Zorbas will be split up. The outside guards will be taken out first. Okay, snipers, tell us how you'd do it."

"Here's the problem." Zorbas said. "Valenzuela and I are going to have to fire at the same time. We'll need a spotter to coordinate our shots. The spotter will have to stopwatch the exact time to fire. If we wound one of the guards, it will alert the other. This isn't going to be easy, but it's doable. Head shots for the guards. What's your opinion, Valenzuela?"

"It's doable, but timing is everything." Valenzuela shifted in his chair. "How close can we get to the cabins without being detected?"

Blackhawk rested his hands on the back of the chair. "I've been within twenty-five yards of the shacks without being seen. Is that close enough?"

Valenzuela looked at Zorbas, then raised his arms like he was aiming a rifle. "At twenty yards, we can shoot the balls off mosquitoes."

"Hot damn," Pharts slapped his thighs. "That's my kinda shootin'. Let's get it on. These dreg SOBs are gonna get their comeuppance."

Pharts' enthusiasm fired up the group. Cassity clapped. I fist pumped, and Kowalski slapped the table in front of him.

"We'll work on the details tomorrow during our mock attack. Let's move on to Paragraph Four—logistics of the operation. Mr. Hopson, can you fill us in?"

Hopson walked to the whiteboard next to Kowalski and motioned for Blackhawk to stand next to him. "We'll have a chopper take the team to a site three miles from the camp on the opposite side of the mountain Blackhawk scouted. You'll rappel by rope at midnight, camp until morning, then Blackhawk will take you to a location a mile from the shacks. We'll have the Chinook pick you up. Any questions?"

"Where's the pickup zone?" Cassity asked.

Hopson hesitated. "Five miles from the still. That's the closest we can land the helicopters. You're on your own until then, but Blackhawk knows the area and the shortest route."

Five miles with the women through rough terrain? The extraction began to look impossible. We'd have a major skirmish with the distillers, too. That was a given.

Pharts raised his hand. "The last time I did a night rappel from a chopper, the pilot dropped us in the middle of a cactus patch. My bum's still got some embedded needles. Can you assure me that won't happen again?"

Hopson laughed, his full mustache giving way to his brilliant smile. "I can assure you there's no cacti in the area."

I didn't know if Hopson chose Pharts for this mission knowing his character would keep us all loose, but I was glad for his sense of humor.

Kowalski took control of the meeting by tapping on the whiteboard. "Paragraph Five—radio frequencies. I'll discuss this tomorrow, but we need to get the challenge and replay code words we'll use in case we get separated. Suggestions?"

Valenzuela stood. "Zorbas and I have that worked out. The challenge word is steel, and the reply word is—"

"Wool." Zorbas' deep voice filled the large room with laughter.

CHAPTER 32

Tick, tick, tick. THE WALL CLOCK IN MY BEDROOM AT THE retreat couldn't have been louder if it had been taped to my skull. I switched on the lamp. The clock read 1:30 a.m. The excitement of the run-through mission later today had kept my adrenalin in overdrive, kicking up too many concerns. What if we were too late and the hostages had been moved? Or Morgan wasn't at the camp? Or they'd already killed her?

Sweat broke out on my face and arms. I popped up. My heart by-passed my chest and pounded straight up my throat. I fluffed the pillow and turned on my right side, needing to stop with the negative thoughts. We had a good team. A solid plan. A plan that was going to work.

Bang, bang, bang. "5 a.m. Let's rock and roll." Kowalski's voice jerked me awake.

At some point, exhaustion must've gotten the best of me because I'd definitely slept.

I flipped back the covers, went into the bathroom, and splashed cold water on my face. I dressed in fatigues, a T-shirt, and combat boots. The smell of bacon pulled me downstairs where the other men were filing into the breakfast area.

The guys were mostly quiet, but small talk about the mission surfaced.

"Kowalski," Pharts said, "are you going to let me recon the area before the actual strike?"

"Yes." Kowalski went for the coffee pot. "We'll talk strategies soon."

"Sounds like a plan." Pharts snapped his fingers. "Let's get some grub."

The breakfast was first class—bacon, scrambled eggs, pancakes, and juice.

Valenzuela broke from the traditional breakfast and drank a Tecate. He said it was another Aztec warrior tradition.

I laughed to myself, wondering just how many *traditions* the guy had.

After breakfast, we headed back to the large living area where two long tables with chairs were set up. Kowalski sat at the end, the whiteboard directly behind him. He picked up a red marker and drew a crude shack on both ends, then labeled the one on the far left *Cabin 1* and the other *Cabin 2*. "Blackhawk told me Worm, the leader, slept inside Cabin 1 the night he stayed at the site. The women were split between 1 and 2."

Hopson's house phone rang and rang before he could get to it. It reminded me of the phone ringing at my house in Belleville before I left for the meeting at the New York warehouse. Had it been Mamma or Tony calling? What were they thinking now? I wished I could've answered that phone and told them what I was doing.

"There are six of us," Cassity interrupted my thoughts. "How are you going to divide the team?"

Kowalski put down the marker and sat. He rested his arms on the table, interlocking his fingers. "We've talked about splitting Zorbas and Valenzuela. We may as well talk about the rest of us. Valenzuela, I'm putting you at Cabin 1. That leaves Zorbas at Cabin 2. After the outside guards are taken out, one man will assault the cabin to get the guard inside. I'll put—"

"Hold on." I stood. "If there's a chance Worm will be in Cabin 1, you're gonna put me there."

"Absolutely." Kowalski leaned back in his chair, crossing his arms. "I thought you'd want that responsibility." He straight-line smiled. "Here's the breakdown I had in mind." He stood and went back to the board, picked up the marker, and wrote *Helmsly, Valenzuela,* and *Pharts* under *Cabin 1. Kowalski, Zorbas,* and *Cassity* under *Cabin 2.* "Is everyone okay with this setup?"

We all nodded.

"Once the outside guards are taken out," Kowalski continued, "the snipers will remain undercover. Pharts, you'll go with Earl, but remain outside and have his back. I'll go inside. Cassity, you'll protect my back. Earl and I will try to capture the men, but will kill if we have to. Snipers, you cover all of us."

After the morning meeting, the team went through a mock-up attack. It appeared to be a fairly easy mission. There were no trained soldiers, and the assault would be a surprise. The difficulty would be coordinating the snipers. Blackhawk said the best time for the rescue would be 3:00 a.m. when the outside guards napped.

Kowalski and I would be spotters to sync our watches at exactly 0300 hours. At that mark, we'd start the stopwatches. We'd wait one minute before the snipers shot the posted guards. That would allow a cushion in case the situation was not ideal for the shots.

Kowalski and I practiced over and over until our timing was spot-on. The snipers used live ammo without suppressors to get a feel for it. Still, if everything went without a glitch, I'd be surprised. There was an old military acronym for things not going as planned—FUBAR. I could feel the pressure mounting. My gut rumbled.

The team practiced the rest of the day on our rescue assignment at the mock-up cabins. We'd leave by helicopter to our drop zone tomorrow night. Failure was not an option.

CHAPTER 33

BUTTERFLIES DIVE-BOMBED MY STOMACH. I STRETCHED OUT ON my bed. I was ready, but pulled out my stopwatch and practiced one more time.

Not an hour later Mr. Hopson showed up at my door. "Earl, are you in there?" Something in his voice was concerning.

"Come in." I gave the recliner to him, then sat in a desk chair, suddenly worried that he wanted to scrub the mission.

Hopson sat and crossed his leg. "I'm stopping by all the guys' rooms and asking if there are any questions before the team leaves."

"How did you find out about Morgan?" I'd wanted to ask earlier, but couldn't find the right time.

"When I hired Blackhawk, he located the moonshine stills and said a woman who matched Dona's description was there. I flew to Gatlinburg. I saw a newspaper article with Morgan's picture. It had both your names and stated you were from Belleville, New Jersey. I asked Blackhawk if a black woman was with my daughter. He said he got a glimpse of one, but didn't see enough to give a full description. I put two and two together and thought the lady at the camp could be Morgan. When I found out you'd been a SEAL, I wanted to give you an opportunity to be on the rescue team. Will you tell me about your wife?"

I eased down into my chair. "She went to the University of Tennessee on a track scholarship and is a two-hundred-meter champion in the Southeast Conference. After her undergraduate degree, she attended the UT Dental School in Memphis. She started her practice in Belleville, New Jersey. That's where I met her." I tapped my jaw. "Toothache."

"I'm going to guess," Hopson said, "a bad tooth was actually a blessing."

"Yes, sir." I grinned. "Morgan's the most beautiful woman I've ever seen. Every time I think of her, my heart beats faster. It's like love on steroids. That's the only way I can explain it." I interlocked my fingers behind my head. Hopson seemed genuinely interested. "My wife's strong-willed. After she was abducted, her momma told me the fools who got her had no idea what they were getting into. And she's right." Thinking about Morgan choked me up. I leaned forward, elbow on my knee, and cleared my throat. "Dona, is she your only child?"

Hopson uncrossed his legs. His eyes widened as any proud father's would. "She's an only child. I married late in life. Dona's mother and I are the same age. After Dona was born, Lynne and I both felt the child-bearing age had passed."

"So tell me, what's Dona like?"

"She's petite and a spitfire. Always has been. One word that describes her is love. Her gift is serving others. A couple of days before Thanksgiving when she was seven, our chauffeur picked her up from school because her mother had bronchitis. I came home from work a little early to bring Lynne medicine. I walked through the back door into the kitchen, and Dona ran to me and grabbed my hand. 'Daddy, I want you to meet my new friend, Gary.' The guy needed a shave six months before I met him. His fingernails were caked with dirt, his coat tattered and dirty, charcoal gray. She told me she saw him by the side of the road and made the chauffeur stop. 'He was hungry so I brought him home and made him a peanut butter and jelly sandwich.'"

I leaned my head back and laughed so hard my lower back ached.

"That's not all," Hopson continued. "Dona said, 'Daddy, Gary doesn't have a job to buy food. I told him you hire lots of people, and you'd give him a job.' That was thirteen years ago. Gary is now caretaker of our estate. He's got six men who work under him and is still Dona's friend."

I looked at Hopson. "I'd be interested to know what you thought of your chauffeur picking up a homeless man."

"I intended to fire him. He told me he considered refusing Dona's request, but a warm feeling spread over him, and he knew everything would be all right."

The more I was around Hopson, the more respect I had for him. For some reason, I thought of my own father. Burl and I never knew him. He died in an auto accident when we were babies. But from stories Mamma told, I had a gut feeling our dad was much like the man across from me.

Hopson walked to the door and put his hand on the knob. "You didn't answer the question I asked when I walked in. Are there any concerns about the mission?"

"Only one." My butterflies returned. "I hope we haven't passed the point of rescue."

CHAPTER 34

THE TEAM PLANNED TO LEAVE HOPSON'S RETREAT AND GO back to his private airport at 9 p.m. I gathered my equipment and checked my weapons, then walked to the front of the house where a van and truck were parked and ready to pick us up.

Hopson gripped my shoulder. "Bring our women home."

The stakes were high, and we both knew it. I gave him a nod and a one-finger salute. "It's a done deal."

The night air seemed heavy. Clouds drifted in front of the full moon. A gust of wind moved tree branches, and swirling leaves brushed against my foot. All we needed was the spine-numbing howl of a werewolf and we'd have the opening of a horror movie.

"Kowalski, did you get a bottle of wolfman repellent?" Pharts echoed my thought.

Kowalski pitched his equipment in the truck, angled his head back, and inhaled twice. "Don't need any. Your body odor should do the trick."

Pharts gave him the up-yours sign.

In the van, the guys talked about sports, politics, and, of course, women. The relaxed mood of the team was a good omen. To me, it signaled we were prepared.

As we approached the airport, the hulking giant CH-47D Chinook helicopter was hard to miss. A formidable piece of equipment, the machine was capable of carrying fifty soldiers and their gear. Overkill for our mission, but one big chopper was better than suddenly needing two to get everyone back. The helicopter had no military markings. It made me wonder what special connections Hopson used to get it. CIA or some other secret organization?

I got out of the van and grabbed my gear from the truck, then marched up the entrance ramp and inside the metal beast.

Everyone boarded except Blackhawk. He stopped about ten feet back, staring at the chopper.

I walked back to meet him. "Is there a problem?"

He didn't answer, but his body resembled a pillar of stone.

"Hey, man, is there a problem?" I repeated.

Arms plastered to his sides, he shook his head. "No way am I getting on that thing."

I chuckled. "Why?"

"I've never been on a helicopter. Doesn't look like it could lift all of us."

"You've never been on a chopper?"

He shook his head and stepped back.

I'd expect someone uneducated to have doubts, but, according to Hopson, Blackhawk was a Yale guy, and he should've known better. "This thing can lift over twenty thousand pounds. If you don't get on, I'm going to a tribal meeting and tell your people you had no guts."

"Okay." Blackhawk sprinted up the ramp all the way inside.

I slapped his shoulder as he ran past. Peer pressure. Worked every time.

As the huge engines of the giant helicopter revved and slowly lifted upward, Blackhawk closed his eyes so tight he had crow's feet forming in the corners.

I couldn't help but laugh and gave him a friendly tap on the shoulder. I'd rappelled dozens of times, so had the others. Blackhawk had practiced from a tall birch tree and caught on quickly. He'd be okay.

According to Hopson, the flight to the drop zone would take about an hour.

I looked out the portal at the full moon. I thought about Morgan—how close I was to her, yet how far away.

The pilot's voice came over the intercom telling us the drop zone was ten minutes away.

I gathered my equipment, put on my rappel gloves, and waited.

The helicopter slowed, then hovered. The drop area was only twenty feet below the aircraft. Kowalski departed first. Blackhawk asked to go next. He wanted out. He had no fear of leaving the chopper, just riding in one. Go figure.

The exits went without a SNAFU. We gathered together to make sure all were okay, checked our gear, and made sure the flashlights worked.

I looked at my watch—12:15—and settled into my sleeping bag, as did the others.

Everyone was quiet. Except for Pharts. He made werewolf howls.

CHAPTER 35

COOL AIR LINGERED OVER THE SMOKY MOUNTAINS AS THE SUN woke me up. The fresh smell of morning dew made me feel alive. Down the mountain, a huge buck — ten points, at least — stood unaware of our presence.

We'd have to forgo morning coffee. Blackhawk estimated a three-to-four mile walk to the moonshine site. We couldn't take a chance of anyone seeing or smelling our campfire.

It was MRE's — Meals Ready to Eat — this morning. They were actually pretty good. Some guys acquired a taste for them and preferred the pouches over prepared meals in the field. My favorite was spaghetti and meatballs. I had no idea how adding water heated the contents. They packed about twelve hundred calories per pouch. A good way to keep going through mid-day.

After breakfast, Blackhawk led us down the mountain. The trees were thick, and the undergrowth slowed our progress. It reminded me how difficult it would be for the women. I tried not to think about escaping the moonshiners. We'd need to get away long before the day workers arrived.

About a mile into the hike, Blackhawk pointed to an open area. A cemetery. Most of the rock tombstones were leaning, and weeds had taken over. We scattered out, looking at the names.

Kowalski called me over. "Look, the tombstone says this was a Confederate soldier. Born — 1849. Died — 1865. He was just a boy. Sixteen."

I put down my rifle, knelt next to the marker, and rubbed my fingers over the engraved name. "Jonathan Collier." I looked up at Kowalski. "When do you suppose the last person was here to see these graves?"

"Your guess is as good as mine." Kowalski poured water on his handkerchief and swiped it across his face. "Some of the headstones have dates in the 1880s. It could've been over a hundred years since someone last saw them."

Everyone except Zorbas was standing over graves.

I motioned to him. "Zorbas, come look at this."

He shook his head. "Ain't no way I'm comin' in that cemetery."

"What?" I said. "Get over here."

"No." Zorbas stood his ground. "Ain't about to walk among all those skeletons. It ain't healthy."

"Are you telling me you're afraid of dead people?" This specimen of a man was freaked out by a cemetery.

Zorbas shook his finger at me. "Don't say that. I'm respectful is all."

Doubted that. But I wasn't going to push the issue with a guy who could beat the life out of me without breaking a sweat. I thought men like Blackhawk and Zorbas wouldn't be afraid of anything. I guess we were all human after all.

We continued to march through the maze of trees until close to sundown. Blackhawk estimated the distance to the moonshiners' camp was no more than a mile on the other side of the mountain.

Blackhawk and Pharts continued on to recon the campsite. They would return with a report the next morning. The rest of us took a much-needed break.

I enjoyed and hated the rest at the same time. Morgan could be just over that mountain. What was she doing? Had she given up hope? Had she tried to escape? No way could I spend time alone right now. I went to Kowalski who sat propped against a tree. "So, tell me about yourself."

"Nothing to tell." He crossed one leg over the other. "Been in the Army since I was eighteen."

I sat across from him on a dead tree stump. "You got family? Tell me about them."

He closed his eyes, then opened them. "Do you really want to know about my family?" His tone was flat and unemotional.

"I need a distraction." I leaned forward, elbows on my knees.

"Don't have any brothers or sisters. We lived in an apartment in Boston. I came home from school when I was seventeen to a twenty-dollar bill and a note on the kitchen table that said Mom was leaving. Dad was a drunk who disappeared for weeks at a time. The rent came due, and I had no money. The manager threw me out. I packed one shirt and a change of underwear and slept in a phone booth for a week. My football coach found out and let me move in with him until the season ended. I turned eighteen and joined the Army. And, here I am."

I paused, staring at him, not knowing what to say. "Did you ever see your mom or dad again?"

He placed a hand over his mouth. His eyes were dead as he slowly shook his head.

I picked up a small pebble and chunked it as far as I could. I stood facing Kowalski. "You've got a brother you don't know about."

He looked up. "What are you talking about?"

I extended my hand, and he reached for mine. I pulled him off the ground. "When all this is over, you'll come to my house, eat at my table, and meet your new family."

Standing toe to toe, our eyes locked, and the dead, dark look he'd had earlier disappeared. He nodded, but never said a word. He didn't have to. We both knew he'd found himself a brother.

CHAPTER 36

I SETTLED IN WITH THE REST OF THE TEAM WHILE PHARTS AND Blackhawk went on to the cabins to gather information vital for a successful mission. The moonshine camp was only a mile away. I imagined just rushing the shacks right now and getting the women out. Fantasy thinking on my part. And reckless. Definitely not the right thing to do. The ladies would be put in more danger without a specific extraction plan.

After the MRE supper, we sat around and shot the bull. Nothing else to do and certainly no campfire. We couldn't even afford to use flashlights, but the full moon gave us plenty of light.

Waiting was the worst part of any mission. Too many potential screw-ups crept into my thoughts. "Embrace and conquer" was the motto of any special ops team. I'd always welcomed the challenge. But, tonight doubts slithered into my brain like a slimy swamp creature. The emptiness of living without Morgan punched me in the gut over and over. I was trained to believe in my skills. I had to fight against the undertow of doubt. I had to get her back.

I fell asleep, but restlessness forced my internal clock to go off. The illuminated hands on my watch showed 0200. I looked around, and everyone slept.

A bird lifted off a branch. The flap of its wings sounded like the whispers of some secret hover craft. Rodents scampered on the dead leaves, reminding me of static on a radio station. The hoot of a far-away owl mimicked a train horn. Life continued on as though nothing abnormal was happening. I would welcome those normal times again. If they ever came.

I laid back down and dozed off. Zorbas and Valenzuela's talking woke me up. I checked my watch — 0500. The recon team should be back before sunup.

At 0530, Pharts and Blackhawk arrived back in camp. After they'd eaten, Kowalski called the team together. "What's the report?"

Pharts unscrewed the lid to his canteen and took a big gulp of water and swallowed. "Pretty much what Blackhawk told us earlier. The women were split up in cabins 1 and 2. One guard inside of each, one outside. They're not being treated well. A woman stumbled over a branch and dropped a case of moonshine. A guard cussed and kicked her in the ribs. It wasn't Dona. Or Morgan." He looked at me. "Got a good look at the guy. Hope he's around when we make the raid. I have plans for him."

He took another swig of water, then wiped his mouth with the back of his hand. "A Coleman lantern sits in front of each building. Lights up the whole area. Once the outside guards are taken out, it'll be no problem seeing to get inside. Oh, and the guards helped themselves to the Mason jars and got pretty looped."

"The outside guards." Kowalski said. "Where are they stationed, and do they still have automatic rifles?"

"Affirmative. Sometimes they're on the porch. Sometimes they sit on a folding chair but never away from the front of the shack." Blackhawk unwrapped a stick of Spearmint gum and stuck it into his mouth.

Kowalski looked at each of us, his stare intense. "The mission's a go. Let's rock and roll."

The time had come. I couldn't control the nervous tingling at my hairline.

"Check your gear and make sure you have everything." Kowalski broke my trance. "We'll leave before the sun goes down and set up position. We attack at 0300."

I checked my weapon and ammo.

Zorbas and Valenzuela made sure their night sights were clean and secure on their rifles.

Cassity snapped his fingers to get Kowalski's attention. "We've got a problem. The field radio's not working."

We all stopped what we were doing. Valenzuela looked at Zorbas. "FUBAR."

"FUBAR," Zorbas spat his tobacco juice.

CHAPTER 37

IF LOOKS COULD KILL, KOWALSKI'D BE ON HIS WAY TO Leavenworth.

"What's the problem?" He walked toward Cassity and kicked at the dirt. He'd probably seen so many things sabotage a mission, he was fed up to his gills.

"I don't know. Everything looks normal. I'd say the batteries are kaput." Cassity messed with the power switch.

Kowalski picked up the radio and did the same thing. Nothing worked. He called the team together. "We'll just have to work this mission with timing. Make sure your watches are synced with mine." His command was spiked with resolve. The mission would not be deterred.

The most important part of the mission was the actual attack, and we'd be fine—as long as the timing was perfect.

We left our campsite mid-afternoon to position ourselves before dark. We'd be in place and concealed for at least nine hours. I didn't know how I'd react if I saw Morgan. Just the thought of her made every nerve in my body twitch. I took deep breaths to relax, but that didn't help. My heart pounded so hard I felt it in my jugular.

The hike through the heavy undergrowth took the immediate focus off Morgan. Halfway to the location, Blackhawk and his team split off and went toward cabin 2.

Pharts led Valenzuela and me to a position near cabin 1, stopping approximately one hundred yards from the shack. He whispered for us to put on the deer musk. When most of the whiskey men went home, we'd move to within twenty-five yards of the still and cabin.

A whiff of sugar water used in distilling caught my attention. Nose candy would be a good way to describe it.

A quickening pinged in my heart and spread through the rest of my body. I was so close to Morgan I could almost taste her soft lips. I had to control the emotions, or I'd risk botching the rescue.

The trees were so thick I couldn't see the building, but I could smell the burning wood that heated water in metal pots. It reminded me of a house fire near us in Belleville. I couldn't describe the scent, but that burned house had a bad lingering effect on me. People died in that fire.

The sun began to sink. Soon I'd be moving into position to strike.

Pharts pointed to his watch, then to the shack, and our team moved out.

I inched closer and closer to taking Morgan home.

Fifty yards from the camp, Pharts raised a fist, the signal to stop. Then he motioned to take cover.

Someone was headed directly toward us.

I pulled my knife. The heartbeat returned to my jugular. Sweat broke out on my arms.

The man stopped within ten feet of Pharts and took the safety off his AK-47. *Click.*

The forest went eerily quiet.

Holding my breath, I tensed, ready to attack, focused on the only part of him I could see—his legs.

"Bo," someone called from the shack. "Where are you? It's time to leave. Come on, man."

The guy didn't move. Then I heard the safety click back on, and he turned and headed back to camp.

Pharts looked at me, puffed his cheeks, and exhaled. To say the encounter was a close call would be an understatement.

After most of the moonshiners left the camp, we took position twenty-five yards from the shack.

A tall, skinny guy backed up to a tree and rubbed his back. I recognized Worm from the spiked blond hair. I wanted to spit to get the taste out of my mouth.

Some of the women were still working, moving the moonshine cases, but I didn't see Morgan. Major disappointment. I supposed she was at the other camp. Maybe it was best I didn't see her. If I had, it might be impossible to contain myself.

Worm and the other guard started drinking about sunset. The blond-haired freak cussed every other word. Illiterate jerk.

I hoped he'd get slobber-mouth drunk. It would make my task easier. But I couldn't let rage cloud my judgment to the point of distraction. Getting Morgan and the other women out safely had to be my focal point.

The guards continued to drink. The more they drank, the more they seemed to harass the women. They taunted them with threats when they didn't retrieve their drinks fast enough and touched them inappropriately.

Worm took particular interest in a woman that looked to be in her twenties. He took her inside the shack.

I wanted to pound my fist on the ground. I couldn't wait to make him pay a price he couldn't afford.

Faces taut, Pharts and Valenzuela had enough hatred blazing in their eyes to start a forest fire.

Worm finally came out alone. And after supper, all the women dragged themselves inside as if moving was an effort, and they'd given up all hope. The guards lit the lantern and sat on the porch and talked, mostly about hunting and drag races.

The night seemed endless.

Around twelve, Worm stumbled to his feet and went back inside the cabin.

The outside guard propped himself up in a folding chair, laid his AK-47 next to him, and lit a cigarette. Unfortunately, he hadn't been drinking that much.

It looked like Valenzuela zeroed in on the guy multiple times.

I couldn't read the sniper's mind, but I think he was ready to perform his mission.

I looked at my watch—0200.

Morgan. I'm coming.

CHAPTER 38

I STARTED GLANCING AT MY WATCH EVERY FEW MINUTES—AS if that would make the time pass quicker. All it did was spike my blood pressure to Mount Everest heights.

Valenzuela rested a few feet away on a pile of needles from a decaying hemlock tree. His demeanor was perfect for a sniper—calm, composed, confident. With his camo hat pulled over his eyes, I couldn't tell if he was awake or asleep.

Nerves tight as a piano string, I couldn't have been calm if I'd been given a bottle of sleeping pills. Earlier I'd wished that Morgan had been in cabin 1, but now I was glad she wasn't. I didn't need the extra pressure.

The group from cabin 2 would meet up with us after the attacks. Blackhawk had said the path to the pickup zone would be easier from our location. Then, I'd be with Morgan.

Five minutes to countdown, I checked my watch and stopwatch for the umpteenth time. Both functioned perfectly.

The guard outside lit his second cigarette in a row. He got up from his chair and stretched, then paced back and forth, rifle dangling by his side, unaware his seconds were numbered.

How easy it would be to take him out right now. I paused and looked at him a little harder. Was he married? Did he have kids? I took no pleasure in taking a life, but he'd made the poor choices that led him here, and circumstances dictated what had to be done.

Three minutes to countdown. The guard walked from the front of the shack to the back, fumbling his zipper. What a time to take a whiz.

When the guard was out of sight, I tapped Valenzuela's shoulder.

He lifted his hat.

I pointed to the cabin.

Two minutes to countdown. Valenzuela positioned his rifle, ready to fire the moment he had the opportunity.

I had a decision to make — wait or go after the guard. I squinted, trying to see around the corner of the cabin. Come on, you SOB. Where are you?

Thirty seconds to countdown.

The guard finally came back.

I started the stopwatch at 0300 and waited a minute before I whispered to Valenzuela. "Five, four, three, two, one."

His bullet exited the barrel with a quiet *poof* that exploded when it smashed into the man's head. Pieces of skull flew in several directions. His body collapsed on the ground with a heavy thud. He never knew what hit him.

I took the safety off my M-16 and sprinted to the front of the cabin and up the rickety porch. The first step squeaked. I stopped, waited, then took another step, careful to make no more noise.

Dona appeared in the window next to the front door.
I raised my index finger to my lips and shook my head.

She pointed to the opposite side of the room where I could barely make out Worm sleeping.

My back pressed against the outside wall, I inched my way to the window opposite Dona and looked inside.

The outside lantern provided more light. I clearly saw Worm on his back, snoring.

I eased my way to the front door, turned the knob, and pushed. The slight whine of the hinges slowed my feet. When Worm didn't move, I eased my way inside.

The other two women in the cabin were awake, huddled in the corner, sharing a thin, faded blanket. Their drawn faces and sunken cheeks reminded me of pictures I'd seen of concentration camp victims from Dachau prison in World War II.

I stared at Worm. What a piece of garbage. I wanted to shoot him on the spot, but a quick death was too easy. Prison time would be hell. A hell he couldn't run from. I picked up Worm's weapon where he'd propped it against the wall next to his bed. "Dona, hold his weapon," I whispered.

Her eyes widened. "How'd you know my name?"

I gave her a quick grin. "Your dad told me."

I could see tension exit her exhausted body as she took the gun.

I touched the tip of Worm's nose with the end of my rifle.

His eyes sprang open like a trap door.

I jammed the barrel into his cheek. "Come on, scumbag, make a move. Give me an excuse."

"Don't shoot, please." He begged for mercy in a whiny voice.

Coward. I looked at his waist. He'd pissed himself. A coward and a wuss.

Someone lit a lantern inside the shack.

I grabbed Worm by his four-inch blond hair and jerked him off the bed. I leaned my rifle against the wall, yanked his arms behind his back, and secured his hands with zip ties.

The women from the corner ran at him like someone had shocked them back to life. They punched, kicked, and slapped him.

And I let them.

One of the ladies grabbed Worm's AK-47 from Dona and pointed it at him.

It was hard not to cheer her on to pull the trigger, but I reminded myself that would be too easy and took the gun from her.

Worm glared at the woman standing closest to him, the same lady he'd dragged into the shack earlier. "You'll pay for this. My men will hunt this guy down, string him up, and gut him like a spring hog, and you'll be next."

She pushed her long hair behind her ears, gritted her teeth, and ran her gaze from Worm's feet all the way to the top of his head, then back down to his waist. Then placed a well-deserved kick to his groin. An NFL kicker couldn't have done it better.

He folded like a wet newspaper, his groans followed by a volley of cuss words.

She bent over Worm until her face came within inches of his. "Why am I the only woman you brought into the cabin?" Her voice was half-whisper, half-low growl. When he refused to answer, she stomped on him.

He pulled his knees to his chest for protection.

The other women hugged each other, their defeated faces finally showing some signs of life.

Outside, the voices of my team brought me back to the mission. To Morgan. Finally, we'd be together.

I grabbed Worm by the shirt, shoved him out the door, and onto the porch in front of the cabin.

The ladies sidestepped us and ran to greet the women from cabin 2.

I stretched, looking for Morgan. Panicked when I didn't see her. Then my gaze locked onto her long brown hair. Her back was to me, and she was talking to Kowalski. Was he telling her I was here?

CHAPTER 39

"MORGAN," I WHISPERED, TURNING MY BRIDE AWAY FROM WHERE she stood in front of Kowalski and pulling her to my chest.

She immediately stiffened.

"It's okay. It's me." I lifted her chin with my index finger.

The lifeless look on her face froze.

Her eyes, the shape of her nose, her chin—none of them were Morgan's. I sucked in a deep breath and stepped back. "Where's the other black lady? Where's Morgan?"

Her eyes fixed on mine, she shook her head. "I'm the only black woman."

I'd waited for this moment. And it had been ripped away. I struggled for air and sprinted toward Worm, grabbed him by the throat.

His eyes bulged.

"Where is Morgan?" I squeezed harder. "Where's my wife?" I demanded.

Valenzuela, Kowalski, and Zorbas pulled on me but couldn't break my grip.

Worm went to his knees.

"Stop it, Earl." Kowalski's voice was eerily calm. "If you kill him, you may never find out."

I turned Worm loose.

He fell backward, fighting to get air. He stumbled to his feet coughing, spitting, and cursing.

I moved away from the group, my emotions spent. Images of Morgan alone and abandoned tortured me.

Worm smirked, his grin and posture cocky.

I ran at him, knocking him to the ground and threw myself on top of him. "You tell me where Morgan is or I'll splatter your brains all over the mountain." I punched him in the face.

"Earl, stop." Kowalski body-checked me, knocking me off Worm. "You can't do this. Get hold of yourself."

Worm gurgled and spat. A bloody snot bubble formed under one nostril. "You're nuts, man. I don't know a Morgan."

Kowalski looked at the women. "Was there another black lady in camp? Her name is Morgan."

They shook their heads.

"I'm so sorry." Dona walked over to me and touched my cheek. "There's never been a woman in the camp named Morgan."

I went numb, defeat draining the fight out of me. Morgan wasn't here. She'd never been here.

"It's not over." Kowalski put both hands on my shoulders. "We'll find her. That's a promise, from one brother to another, but right now we have to move out. It'll be light soon, and the moonshiners will be looking for us. Are you with me?"

I nodded and placed a shaky hand over my eyes.

Kowalski gently shook my shoulders. "Good. We need you. Some of the women don't have proper shoes or clothing to make it out of here. Will you help distribute the clothing we brought?"

All I could do was nod again.

The teams only captured one guard, Worm. At cabin 2, Zorbas killed the outside guard as planned, but had to shoot the other one when he tried to escape.

After the women changed, Kowalski brought everyone together. "Blackhawk will guide us to the pickup point. Ladies, two of you will tie the end of a rope around your waist. The rest of you latch on to prevent anyone from being lost. Any volunteers?"

Dona raised her hand. "I'll do it."

"So will I," another lady spoke up.

"We've no time to waste." Kowalski secured the rope around Dona and the other lady. The rest took hold. "Dona, you follow Blackhawk. Men, use your flashlights and spread among the women."

The five miles to the pickup zone through this forest would be problematic. We'd have to fight our way out. There was no way we could outpace the moonshiners.

Darkness and the thick honeysuckle made walking difficult, but the women were troopers. They pushed through the growth without complaining. About two hours into the escape, the sun broke over the mountains. The women were exhausted. We took a ten-minute break.

Kowalski gathered the team away from the women. "We're not making good time. Cassity, you'll have to stay behind and slow down the moonshiners. You have the coordinates to the pickup zone. You'll have to get back on your own. You okay with that?"

Cassity opened his backpack and pulled out the hand grenades and tripwire. "I'll set a trap for the bloody fools," his voice chock-full of confidence.

Pharts walked to Cassity and took the grenade from his hand. "I'll stay with him. You know the Irish. They can't read a compass." Pharts did his best to imitate Cassity's Irish twang.

Cassity cocked his head and flipped him the bird.

Kowalski smiled and nodded.

I'd bet my last dollar he had great respect for both men. Those two were putting their lives on the line for all of us.

"Everyone ready?" Kowalski grabbed his pack. "Time to move on."

Dona approached Kowalski. "Sir, let me introduce the other women."

He seemed embarrassed. It was as though he totally forgot the human element of courtesy. "Of course, I'm sorry."

"No need for apologies. We haven't had time. We all understand." Dona's words were spoken with appreciation.

Kowalski motioned for the team to come over. "Hey guys, come meet the ladies."

We lined up as though a commanding officer was doing an inspection.

Dona introduced each lady. "This is Sue, Casey, Sandra, Barbara, and Kelly."

Each woman hugged our necks.

I wished for Morgan to hug mine. I had to close my eyes to hold back the rush of emotion.

"Aw, that's so sweet." Worm's tone was riddled with sarcasm. "Too bad all you pricks are gonna be dead by tomorrow. And as for you ladies...let's just say, you don't have a clue what's gonna happen to you."

Zorbas shouldered his rifle, opened his pouch of Red Man, stuffed his mouth, and walked like John Wayne toward Worm. He leaned in close. "We might not get out of here alive, but I promise you, my last bullet is going right between your eyes." Zorbas tapped Worm on the forehead. Then he took a step back and delivered an elbow into Worm's face. His shattered teeth bounced like popcorn in an open pan. Blood gushed from the corner of his torn lip.

In the last few hours Worm had been kicked in the groin, strangled, and pounded in the face. He looked like fresh ground beef with splotches of purple bruises.

And I enjoyed every minute of his pain.

CHAPTER 40

I YANKED WORM OFF THE GROUND, AND HIS KNEES BUCKLED as he tried to balance himself. In a mock gesture of civility, I dusted the leaves off his shirt and tugged on his bruised cheek. "You ready to go, tough boy?" Gathering the rope the women used, I made a hangman's noose and slipped it around his neck.

He shook, his eyes widening.

I should just string him up right there. Instead, I handed the rope to Kelly and told her to secure it around her waist. "Worm, you try and make a run for it, she'll pull you down like a rodeo calf."

Kelly tied the rope and gave it such a good tug that Worm had to take a step to keep from falling.

Blackhawk shouldered his rifle, adjusted his cap, and walked to Kowalski. "The moonshiners are gaining faster than I thought. We'll never get the women to the pickup zone safely at this rate. If the mountain men capture any of us, a bloodbath will follow. Making a stand is our only hope. There's an open area close by. It's a good fifty yards across and another fifty deep—the perfect place for an ambush."

Kowalski stroked his five o'clock shadow. "Earl, when we get to the clearing, gag Worm with the duct tape, then break off to the left. Valenzuela and Zorbas will take the right. Blackhawk and I will secure the middle. We'll catch 'em in with crossfire. Don't shoot until you hear my M-60 burst. If we can't contain the moonshiners, leapfrog behind me with the women. I'll cover, then leapfrog behind you. Let's move out."

The tough-minded ladies insisted on helping. Kowalski gave them the task of handing him the ammo can for the M-60 machine gun.

The open area, devoid of trees, was an ideal kill zone. We moved into position, the hot, noon sun directly overhead.

Four hawks circled, the updraft so strong they didn't have to flap their wings. Did they know something we didn't? Were they waiting to feast on our flesh? If only I could see what they saw. I closed my eyes for a few erratic heartbeats, struggling to reign in my anxiety. Silent, almost not breathing, I listened to the *tum-tump, tum-tump* of my heart against my chest.

Without warning, the crisp *plop* of a bullet leaving the short-barreled AK-47 rang out.

I flinched and scoped out where the shot had come from. One of two things had to have happened. Either the booby trap with the grenades didn't work, or Cassity and Pharts were discovered before the trap was set. Neither were good. Especially since I hadn't heard return fire from their M-16s.

A quickening exploded in my middle and expanded outward, heating my limbs and hardening my hatred. If those sorry SOBs executed my teammates —.

Payback dominated every thought I had. I dropped to my stomach, hidden by a pink-and-white flowering bush so thick I had to break away part of the growth to see.

The rest of the team was camouflaged, poised and ready.

Twenty minutes passed.

Sweat broke out on my forehead. I heard talking as the moonshiners approached the forest opening.

Fifteen men broke into the open area. Bunched up like that, those poor bastards made it easy. Their loud talking indicated they had no idea a trap was set. They moved closer.

Fifty yards.

Forty.

Thirty.

Twenty.

Ten.

And they walked directly in front of Kowalski and Blackhawk.

My fingertips tingled. Come on, Kowalski. Fire.

The buzz-saw machine gun opened up. Pieces of flesh ripped away from the moonshiners' bodies. Blood splattered like drops of rain hitting the pavement. Screams echoed through the trees.

At least ten men crumpled on the ground, their bodies twisted like pretzels. Three men sprinted for cover directly toward me. Others broke toward Valenzuela and Zorbas.

I waited until I could see the fear etched into their faces before I fired — *rat-tat-tat, rat-tat-tat*.

Lifeless bodies crumpled in front of me.

One man broke for the woods.

I fired three rounds, each in a tight pattern.

Bullseye. He fell face forward.

The smell of gun powder filled the air behind me, and the smell of death came from in front of me, strong and putrid and nauseating.

The team gathered in the middle of the field, weapons ready, while we checked the bodies.

I'd experienced slaughterhouse scenes like this with flesh scattered in bits and pieces around me. But I never got used to it.

Kowalski dropped to one knee. He looked at the carnage, turned his head to one side, and spat. "It doesn't look good for Cassity and Pharts. Who's in the search party?"

Valenzuela jammed new rounds in his sniper rifle. "I'll go."

"Me, too." Zorbas checked his cargo pants and pulled out a handful of ammo.

"Blackhawk, how far to the pickup zone?" Kowalski asked.

"Best estimate, one to two miles." He pointed in the direction of the helicopter pad.

Kowalski wiped the dust off his watch. "We've got a couple of hours before the chopper arrives. It's a good thing we had a predetermined plan before we lost radio communication. We should have no problem meeting the deadline."

Across the clearing, Worm and the women headed toward us, the ladies' arms folded across their chests and their heads down as if that could keep out the disturbing bloodbath.

Worm looked at his dead comrades with no expression. No emotion. It was as though he was staring at an open space, and the men meant nothing to him.

I took the safety off my rifle and placed my finger on the trigger. For a split second, I saw myself shooting him. My hand shook with the need to make that image a reality. Before I lost control, I clicked my safety on and removed my finger from the trigger. I was better than him. I was. I had to be for Morgan.

The women circled the bodies, arms still tight across their chests.

Months of counseling were in store for each of them. Some might never fully recover from their horrible ordeal.

I thought of Morgan, not knowing where she was. She was barbed-wire tough, but how long could she hold on?

"Let's move out." Kowalski shouldered his weapon and pointed to Blackhawk to lead the way. Facing Valenzuela and Zorbas, he said, "We'll send some of the rescue crew to help with the bodies."

Both nodded and headed back into the woods.

I let the group get a few yards ahead of me. "Morgan, where are you?" I whispered.

CHAPTER 41

THE PATH TO THE CHOPPER TOOK US THROUGH HIGH BRUSH areas again, making the steep climb difficult.

As I watched the women press forward, I was proud to be a part of the rescue mission. Proud I'd been part of destroying the cartel of evil. Proud to send Worm to jail.

"Thank you for saving us." Dona left the front of the line to join me, her smile kind. "Who were the men who went to set the traps?"

"Pharts and Cassity." I scratched the side of my face. Thoughts of my teammates cast a shadow on the mission.

"Do you think they're okay?"

"I don't know." I wanted to have hope, but hope vanished like a spring mist. My buddies weren't coming back, and Morgan hadn't been at the camp.

Dona cleared her throat and wiped her eyes. "I wish your wife had been with us. There's nothing I can say except don't give up hope. I'm sure she's strong and knows you're looking for her. Just like I knew my dad was looking for me. That kept me alive. It'll keep her alive too."

I couldn't see my smile, but I could feel it. It wasn't real like Dona's. It belonged on someone else's face. Because I'd never really smile again without Morgan.

"It's a good thing you found us when you did. There was talk around camp we were being moved tomorrow." She grabbed my arm and squeezed, like she needed to be sure I was real, the rescue was real, and we were taking her to safety.

Our conversation continued as we hiked. I felt a bond with Dona. She was a good, caring person. Just like her dad.

We'd been walking about an hour and a half when the muffled sounds of helicopter blades cut through the air in the distance. Right on schedule.

Blackhawk removed his cap and circled it overhead, then did a few Cherokee dance moves.

The women hugged each other.

Warmth spiraled through my tired body. Mission accomplished. Almost. An image of Morgan flashed before me.

Two hundred yards ahead, the huge CH-47D Chinook helicopter landed.

Kowalski took the rope from Kelly and led Worm to the open area.

Easing next to him, I gave a not-so-friendly slap on the back of his head and pointed to the aircraft. "You're gonna love the ride on that big boy. I'll save you a seat next to me."

Worm turned his head. He looked like someone had taken a leak on the front seat of his brand-spanking-new shiny, red convertible.

The helicopter crew had sandwiches and drinks ready for us, and we relaxed for thirty minutes. I sat on a stump facing Kowalski, my back to the woods.

He took a bite of his ham and cheese, then laughed so hard chunks of the sandwich fell out of his mouth.

"What's the deal, man?"

He pointed over my shoulder to the woods, then stood, lifting both arms high over his head.

I turned.

Pharts, Cassity, Zorbas, and Valenzuela walked in like they'd been on a stroll in the park.

All I could do was stare. No way, not in a zillion years, did I think Pharts and Cassity would be alive after their encounter with the moonshiners.

I jogged over, opened my arms, and pulled them in. "How in the heck did you two make it out alive? I heard the AK-47 open up, but no return fire."

Pharts took his backpack off, plunked it next to the Chinook, and scratched his privates. "Got any cold golden nectar?"

Kowalski tossed him a can of beer.

Pharts popped the top. Foam spewed all over his dirty, stubbled face. He didn't even wipe it off. "You want the short version or the long one?"

"Short." Kowalski and I bellowed in unison. The Cajun could be long-winded.

Pharts sat with his back against the chopper wheel, legs bent, gripping his golden nectar. He tilted the can back and with two large gulps finished the beer. He belched. It sounded like a horn on a luxury liner. "Got another one?"

Kowalski's grin stretched with amusement. "Not until you tell your story."

Another burp followed, not as loud, but with a mellow baritone ring. "Cassity's such a perfectionist.

We leaned our rifles against a tree and set the tripwire. Then he says, 'I think the moonshiners will probably come through this area, but twenty feet to our left.' So we untie the wire and moved it to another tree. And wouldn't you know, we didn't take our rifles. I guess the 'shiners sent out a recon scout. Anyway, this goofy, flop-eared hillbilly spots us, and all we could do was run like scalded dogs into the woods. The guy fired, but missed. He didn't try to chase us down. I guess he figured the women and Worm were a bigger prize. It's Cassity's fault. If we hadn't moved the tripwire, we'd have had our rifles to fire back."

Cassity waved his hands back and forth. "Ya bloody Cajun. That's so much BS. I told you to get the rifles. My hands were full of grenades and wires." He leaned his head back and laughed.

Pharts took a swig of beer and wiped his mouth with the back of his hand. "Next thing I know, these two big dudes walk up." He pointed to Zorbas and Valenzuela. "And here we are."

Kowalski scrunched his nose. "Okay, guys, do you think Pharts deserves another beer?"

"No." We all shouted and chunked our empties at him.

He scurried under the chopper.

I looked at the women. When we first rescued them, they were relieved. Now, after that bloodbath they witnessed, they were withdrawn and huddled together. I heard one of them ask with contempt what was going to happen to Worm.

The look on Worm's ugly face reminded me of watching someone swallow castor oil.

After the short break, we loaded our gear and prepared to take off. The pilot radioed Max Hopson to have the authorities waiting at the Newfound Gap parking lot along with ambulances to take the women to the hospital.

I hard-checked Worm down on the seat next to me.

He gawked at me, one eye almost swollen shut. "Can you loosen the plastic tie? My hands are numb."

I fake smiled. "Sure."

He leaned forward.

I grabbed both wrists with one hand and ratcheted the band tighter with the other. "Is that better?"

He leaned back, gritting his teeth.

After the short flight to Newfound Gap, a squad of park security and ambulance personnel greeted us.

I helped Dona exit the chopper.

When she saw her father, she ran to him, tears streaming down her face.

The reunion warmed my heart. And swallowed it whole at the same time. I wanted it to be Morgan running into my arms.

Max held Dona, their bodies rocking sideways. He saw me standing by myself, and they walked over. "Thank you for bringing my daughter back. I'm sorry Morgan wasn't at the camp. I'll do whatever I can to help you find her." He gave me a firm slap on the shoulder. "Let's meet in the morning. We'll make a plan." He took my hand, and his handshake was firm, backing up his promise.

"Earl." Leroy Shannon approached me. "The FBI will interrogate the prisoner about his operations, and I'll make sure they keep me in the loop. Just because Morgan wasn't in the camp with the other ladies doesn't mean he doesn't know of her whereabouts."

All I could do was nod and look at the women we *had* rescued. They were just ordinary people until men like Worm shattered their lives. I couldn't make sense of their twisted, warped minds, but justice would be served. I'd see to that.

I entered the chopper to get Worm. We were the last to exit the aircraft. "When we get off the ramp, I'll cut you loose so the authorities can cuff you. You're going to lie face down on the pavement and extend your arms straight out. If you so much as move a finger, I'll bury my foot so deep it'll take a surgeon to remove it. Do you understand?"

He nodded and knelt on both knees, then belly-flopped.

I cut the plastic tie.

He stretched out his arms to be cuffed.

A tattoo of a black widow spider was inked on the web of his right hand. I'd seen that tattoo before. On another person in Gatlinburg. "You worthless piece of scum." I stomped his hand twice, the bones snapping like brittle chicken wings. Ignoring his loud screams, I took off toward Shannon. "Give me your truck keys."

"What?" He looked puzzled.

"Just give me your keys. Please."

He pulled them from his pocket and handed them to me.

I sprinted to his pickup and peeled out of the parking lot.

CHAPTER 42

I SPED DOWN THE MOUNTAIN FROM NEWFOUND GAP TO Gatlinburg, almost losing control of the pickup. Keep calm. Slow down. Don't kill yourself now. Not when you finally know who can tell you where Morgan is.

I pulled into the parking lot of Maw Tuttle's Last Chance Store, the place where we'd bought our camping supplies. I slammed on the brakes, got out of the truck, not bothering to close the door, and busted into the building. My combat boots clobbered the old, wooden floors.

Maw Tuttle stepped from behind the curtain that separated the store from her living quarters. The second she saw me, she reached behind the door frame and pulled out a rifle.

Before she could shoulder the gun, I yanked it from her. Placing one hand around Maw's throat, I squeezed. "Where. Is. My. Wife?"

"I don't know what you're talking about." Her words were barely audible.

"I'm giving you one more chance before I snap your scrawny neck. Where is she?" My grip tightened.

Her face turned a purplish-red. Veins popped on her forehead. She pointed to a door.

I shoved her toward it, gripping her neck with one hand and holding the rifle in the other. "Open it."

She fumbled for the key in the pocket of her red-and-black plaid apron. Her feeble hand slid the key into the lock and opened a door that led to a cellar.

I pulled an extension cord from the wall socket and tied her hands behind her back then used another cord to tie her to a heavy oak table.

The metal cellar door made a screeching noise that could've been part of a horror-movie soundtrack. My heart pumped so hard I felt it in my neck.

My steps sounded hollow on the rickety wooden stairs. At the bottom, I saw Morgan sitting on the edge of a cot. Her gray cotton warm-ups clung loosely to her drooped shoulders. Her brown hair hung limp. And the fingernails she always kept perfectly painted were chipped.

A musty smell filled the room, and the cracked concrete floor looked damp and cold. A small lamp in the corner of the room barely highlighted her tired body.

As she looked up, my heart stopped, then restarted. She stared at me with no emotion. It was as though she couldn't decide if I was really here or I was just a dream.

"Morgan." I made my voice soft and reassuring. "It's me." I stood the rifle in the corner of the room.

She slowly lifted her body off the cot. Her first steps were slow and cumbersome, then she ran toward me. Grabbing me around the neck, she sobbed so hard her body shook.

I eased her head off my chest and kissed her. "It's okay. I'm here." The long-awaited moment was surreal.

I wrapped my arms around her again, holding her tight. The warmth of her body radiated through my chest. Tears of happiness clouded my vision. I kissed the top of her head.

She cried and cried.

I waited until she stopped before I eased her head off my chest and smiled. "We're going back to Newfound Gap. A medical team and park rangers are waiting for us. Maw Tuttle's tied up at the top of the stairs. She'll never hurt you again, I promise. Are you okay to walk up the stairs?"

She nodded.

I helped her up the stairs anyway.

Maw Tuttle glared at us. I'd seen that glare before when Worm had looked at the dead moonshiners. She was a cold-blooded, pathetic human being with no empathy for human life. She squinted, and the wrinkles around her eyes deepened. "How did you know I had her? Did my son tell you?"

I bent down, my eyes level with her. "No, Worm didn't tell me."

"Then how did you know?" Her voice was as monotone as her stare.

I pointed to the web between her index finger and thumb. "Both of you have exactly the same tattoo. I noticed yours the day we bought camping supplies for our honeymoon."

Her eyes bugged out like a bull frog. "Is that all you had to go on?"

My smile was menacing. "How many people in Gatlinburg would have that same tattoo on the same body part?" I gave her a mocking pat on the head. "Give me a little credit." I hesitated. "One question. Why did you pick Morgan?"

Maw didn't answer.

Morgan tugged on my arm. "I'll tell you when we get outside."

We headed to the front door of the building.

"Hey, I need to go to the bathroom," Maw yelled to us.

I slowly turned to face her, shrugging my shoulders. "Why are you telling me? Go right ahead."

I helped Morgan get into the pickup on the driver's side and slid in beside her. She grabbed my arm so tight I could barely shove the key into the ignition.

As we pulled out of the parking lot, she began to cry again, sobs so loud and heavy they had to come from the bottom of her soul. Every time she managed a breath, she'd start all over again.

I wrapped my arm around her shoulders and pulled her tight. "It's okay, let it out."

When her sobs finally slowed, she wiped her cheeks with the sleeve of her dirty sweatshirt. "The first day of my capture, four men dragged me from our camp. They tied a rug around me and cinched it with a rope. They said the heavy carpet would hide my scent from the search-and-rescue dogs." She bent over and put a hand over her mouth and cried again.

I rubbed her back. "I've got you back. That's all that matters."

"One of the men went ahead. I suppose to warn us if someone was coming. About midafternoon, the scout said two men and a tracking dog were headed our way.

We were about twenty yards below the trail. This Worm guy lay on top of me and pushed a rag into my mouth. The dog pulled off the trail. That's when I saw you. The dog was coming toward me. He had my scent. I know he did. The other man pulled the bloodhound back, and then you were gone."

I slammed my fist into the steering wheel over and over. I remembered Jake, the bloodhound, pulling hard on the leash. Why hadn't I insisted Shannon let the dog do his job? I sucked in air through my teeth. I was furious. "Why did Maw choose you?"

Morgan drew in a deep breath and exhaled. "Some rich guy from the Middle East wanted a certain woman—a tall, mellow-skinned black woman with blue eyes. Maw was so proud she could accommodate the SOB. Like I was her blue-ribbon Angus."

I slammed on the brakes and pulled over. "You were going to be sold into slavery?"

Morgan eyes bore into mine. Then she closed them. "The man was supposed to fly in last week and pick up his...property." She stumbled over the word. "But his jet had engine trouble. Maw said I was scheduled to leave tomorrow." She placed a hand on my face and rubbed back and forth. "Thank you for saving me."

I lowered my head, thanking God for his mercy. "The authorities will want your account of what happened, then we have some phone calls to make to our family." I pulled the pickup back onto the road and headed to Newfound Gap—the first step in taking my wife home.

CHAPTER 43

THREE WEEKS AFTER WE'D GOTTEN HOME, MORGAN ROLLED over and screamed in bed. "Untie me." She turned hitting and scratching my face. "Let me go."

"Morgan...Morgan, it's okay. I'm here." I pulled her close. "It's okay." This wasn't a new occurrence. The abduction had taken its toll.

Her frightened heart beat like a kettle drum against me, her T-shirt was soaked, and her face was hot and wet. She calmed down but didn't talk. After a few minutes, she fell asleep.

The morning sun broke through the curtain in our bedroom, waking me. I reached for her, but she wasn't there. I heard dishes rattle in the kitchen and found her staring out the window over the kitchen sink. She squeezed and released her coffee cup while steam drifted off the top and disappeared.

"Good morning." I wasn't sure what else to say or how she would react. I didn't always know the best way to help.

My greeting went unanswered, but she took her cup and sat at the kitchen table.

I poured a cup of coffee and sat across from her. "How about a jog? I think I can smoke you in a two-mile run."

"I told you yesterday, I don't want to run." Morgan turned her head, her eyes blank as though she was removed from reality.

I took a sip of coffee. "But you love jogging, and you always beat me when we race."

She slammed the table. Coffee from both mugs splattered everywhere. "I hate running now. Don't ask me again." Her tone was filled with a venom I didn't deserve and certainly didn't understand. It was like she'd totally switched off emotionally with little regard for anyone. And even less for herself.

This wasn't the woman I married. But really, who could blame her? I had to be understanding. Her therapist had warned us about flashbacks and rants. Thank God her mom and my family understood the healing process better than I did. She needed someone to get her through this.

Every time she had a nightmare or got angry or refused to do the things she loved, it ripped my heart open. I still blamed myself every day for leaving her at the campsite. I'd rarely let her out of sight the last few weeks. And that was driving her crazy too. But I had to be patient. I had to.

CHAPTER 44

With counseling sessions and time, Morgan improved week by week. She started back to work at the Brady Dental Clinic and felt secure enough to do her daily activities without me, but she never went anywhere by herself at night.

We finally started jogging again, and she beat me regularly. Her infectious smile returned. Her impish giggle was back. Her confidence was evident. I could see improvement. The therapist told us the memory would always be with her, but as the days went on, she should be able to manage the trauma.

The trial for Maw Tuttle and her son Worm was scheduled in two weeks at a federal court in Knoxville. How would my wife handle seeing the Tuttles? Only time would tell.

CHAPTER 45

THE DECEMBER WEATHER IN BELLEVILLE WAS COLD, WET, AND dreary. Dreary matched our mood. Four months after Morgan's abduction, the trial date for Maxine (Maw) Tuttle and Chuckie (Worm) Tuttle had finally arrived.

I leaned back against the kitchen counter and loosely crossed my arms. "Honey, how do you feel about going back to Tennessee?" She was scheduled to testify in less than a week.

"You're really asking if I'm going to draw back into a shell, afraid to face the Tuttles. Isn't that right?" She put down the plate she was drying.

I nodded, terrified that reliving her kidnapping would awaken old demons we'd barely put to bed.

Morgan pointed her index finger at me. "You get this straight. I will never, ever kowtow to those half-wits. I want you to make me a promise. If I make a run at either of those two, stop me from ripping their throats out. Do you copy?"

I smiled like a kid with a new bike. "Yes, ma'am. I copy." My wife was on her way back to her old, fighting self.

The first day of the trial was cold and windy. Christmas decorations draped around the street lights in Knoxville, whipping in a frenzy as we walked into a courthouse that looked like it'd been built in the 1930s.

The marbled floors and ornate oak wood trim sparkled under the bright ceiling lights giving it a stately appearance. The old wooden theater-type chairs were in mint condition as though they'd been carefully restored. I wondered how many lives had been changed for better or worse inside these four walls.

The courtroom was full. The case had been front and center in the news for days.

My brothers, Burl and Tony, sat next to my sisters, Mary Nelle and Belinda, in the back. Jim Pepperman was right in the middle of them. They'd left the hotel early to get a seat. We'd had a good visit the night before, and I was glad to have their support.

Mamma and Morgan's mom made their way to the second row. Next to them were Lynne and Max Hopson. Dona and the other five ladies had taken their seats on the first row behind the prosecutor's table. Morgan slipped in by Dona. With the aisle seat vacant, I sat by Morgan.

Butterflies kamikazed my stomach. Mostly for Morgan. But she seemed focused. Game-day focused and ready to kick tail. Even if her face was a little tense, she put on the appearance of being rock solid. Her shoulders high and her chin up, she pumped her crossed leg as if she couldn't wait to testify.

Maw Tuttle and Worm entered with their lawyer. It was hard to recognize either of them. Maw had on a beige dress, and her gray bun had been replaced by a short, curly cut that took her from country to city.

Worm's spiked-hair was now parted and average length. His starched white shirt and solid red tie were obvious window dressing for the jury. But nice clothes couldn't take the evil out of his eyes.

Morgan glared at her captors, her leg pumping faster.

Did she want to run or did she want to strangle those monsters? My bet was on the latter.

Worm looked over his shoulder at the gallery behind him. He did a double-take, then slowly turned facing the bench. His face went as white as a roll of toilet paper.

I leaned forward to see what he saw.

On the row directly behind the defense table sat the rescue team—Kowalski, Zorbas, Valenzuela, Pharts, and Cassity. Kowalski gave me an index-finger salute.

I chuckled softly. Now I knew the reason for Worm's pale coloring. He'd probably messed himself. Hope he had.

Assistant U.S. Attorney Hanna Karlsson, who represented Morgan, Dona, and the other ladies, walked in. A former professor at University of Tennessee College of Law, she was tall and dressed in a navy pin-striped suit and spiked heels. The way her short, blonde hair swept back from her face completed her powerful, take-charge image. I'd guess she was in her late thirties.

Hanna had talked with Morgan on the phone several times before coming to New Jersey to see us. We liked her. Better yet, we trusted her because she was upfront about exactly what to expect during the trial.

"Oyez, oyez, oyez." The bailiff stood to the side of the court bench. "The United States Court for the Eastern District of Tennessee, the Honorable Debby Dozer presiding, is now in session. God save the United States and this Honorable Court. All rise."

Silence drifted over the room in respect of the court.

The door to the right of the bench opened. A silver-haired woman in a black robe entered. Her small wire-framed glasses gave her a scholarly look. An Ohio native known for her no nonsense approach in criminal cases, she was supposedly as tough as a Marine Corps drill instructor.

"Take your seat." Judge Dozer sat, then addressed us. "The case before the Court is a criminal case, the United States of America vs. Maxine Tuttle and Chuckie Tuttle."

Her statement got my attention. A lump formed in my throat, and I swallowed hard. The entire country versus the Tuttles. Pride built in my chest and spread through my body.

"The government is represented by Assistant United States Attorney Hanna Karlsson, and the Defendants are represented by Paul Bryan of the law firm Perry, Perry, and Mason." The judge continued. "The charge against the defendants is human trafficking."

The jury was chosen and seated in the jury box.

Judge Dozer asked the bailiff to swear them in and then asked the attorneys if they were ready.

Both stated yes.

Hanna Karlsson rose from her chair and approached the bench. "Good morning, Your Honor. I'm Hanna Karlsson, representing the government in this case." Her spine stiff as a steel support beam, she walked toward the jury like a four-star general about to address her troops. She placed her fingertips together, forming a triangle, and paused for a good fifteen seconds.

Not one person in the courtroom moved.

"My job is to prove beyond a reasonable doubt that a crime was committed against these women." Hanna extended her hand to them. "Morgan Helmsly, Dona Hopson, Sue Scarborough, Casey White, Sandra Whitmire, Barbara Dunlap, and Kelly Jordan. A heinous crime so brutal the world will shudder with disgust once they hear the details. Morgan Helmsly was held in the basement of a building in Gatlinburg, snatched from her family with no idea of her whereabouts or if she was still even alive. The other women were held in a camp deep in the Smoky Mountains waiting to be sold overseas in the exploitive slave practice of human trafficking, an international crime against human rights and human freedom."

The jurors hung on Hanna's every word. When she paced, every eye followed her. Morgan and I were no exception.

"Exhibit A." Hanna picked up a notebook from her table. "This ledger was found during a search of the Tuttles' property. It shows the sales of human lives overseas for the last five years. Young women found in Nashville, Chattanooga, and Knoxville." She gripped the book tighter.

"I'm going to prove Maxine Tuttle and Chuckie Tuttle were recruiters for human trafficking and that my clients were their victims, subjected to forced labor until they could be sold. These ladies, with the exception of Morgan Helmsly and Dona Hopson who were abducted, came to the Tuttles after being promised a better life. They had been living off the street, surviving the best they could." She leaned closer to the jury, catching every single one of their stares. "They were offered housing, clothes, and money. Lots of money to move overseas. It didn't take the women long to realize they'd been lied to. Once they got deep in the Smoky Mountains, they were forced into labor at the camp distillery and were unable to leave. Guards at the camp told them they were being sold into slavery." Returning to her seat, she placed her forearms on the table and interlocked her fingers.

Her opening statement prickled the skin on the back of my neck.

The defense was next. The Tuttles had hired the law firm of Perry, Perry, and Mason from New York City. This group was well-known for getting the rich and famous out of jams. The lead attorney was tall and slender with an athletic build. His black hair was slicked back, and the courtroom lighting reflected off the oily texture. Large, pointed ears held the lawyer's black-framed glasses in place.

Morgan poked me in the ribs. "He couldn't look more like Lucifer if he tried."

I smiled on the inside.

"Your Honor, I'm Paul Bryan, representing Maxine and Chuckie Tuttle." He adjusted the cuffs of his blue oxford shirt. "The government has tried to paint a lurid picture of my clients, and they want you to think these women were victims." He also gestured to the women, but in a curt, dismissive motion.

"The government said the Tuttles were involved in human trafficking. The truth is the Tuttles have never even heard of human trafficking. They thought they were doing these ladies a favor by arranging overseas flights to set them up in better lives. These ladies were living off the street, barely able to afford to eat." His high-pitched voice and northern accent made me cringe.

Morgan leaned forward in her seat to get up.

"Hanna said this would happen." I forced her down in her chair. "Give her the chance to correct the jury when it's her turn."

Morgan grabbed my arm and squeezed so hard her body shook.

The first few days of the trial were the same. A lot of back-and-forth verbal jousting. A lot of me keeping Morgan in her seat. And a lot of Morgan putting my arm in a chokehold.

As Hanna called each of the victims to the stand to tell their stories, the jury members nodded in sympathy. Unfortunately, when the Tuttles' lawyer cross-examined the ladies, the jury nodded too. The guy was as much of a worm as Worm.

At the end of day five, Morgan stormed through the door of our hotel suite and picked up a sofa cushion and hurled it across the room. "How can any person with a moral conscience defend people like the Tuttles?"

"First of all, that weasel obviously has no moral conscience. And second, it's his job." I guided her to a chair and put my arms around her tense shoulders. "I know you're upset, and so am I. It's all I can do to keep my composure, but that's the way our legal system works."

Morgan started to interrupt.

"But Hanna's doing a great job." I rubbed her shoulders. "I've watched the jurors. She's winning the arguments. No question about it." I wasn't as sure as I sounded, but in no way would I give credence to the defense attorney. Morgan couldn't handle that.

She rocked back and forth in the chair, her face cupped in her hands. "I don't think I could stand it if the Tuttles weren't found guilty." She backhanded a tear. "That's not possible, is it?"

"They'll pay for their crimes. Trust our justice system. We gotta have faith." Again, I wasn't so sure. Hanna had said that trafficking was a low-risk crime with high profit due to lack of adequate legislation, and that many cases were dismissed because it was hard to prove the victims didn't willfully participate. I couldn't help but think what it would do to Morgan if the Tuttles were found not guilty.

CHAPTER 46

TODAY WAS THE DAY MORGAN WAS SLATED TO GIVE HER testimony.

I'd sat in on the preparation session she and Hanna had when we first got to Knoxville. Notepads, pens, and loose-leaf papers had been strewn all over the place, Hanna's groundwork extensive. She'd gone over the questions she would ask, what the defense could do with rebuttal, and how Morgan should respond. But none of that took away the sinking feeling in my gut. I wasn't sure I could listen again to what happened to my wife.

We'd only been in our seats ten minutes when the day's proceedings began, and I already wanted a break.

Hanna stood and addressed the bench. "Your Honor, may I proceed with my last witness?"

"You may call your witness."

"The prosecution calls Morgan Helmsly to the stand."

Morgan's walk to the witness box was powerful — her steps measured and precise — but as she sat and ran her fingers through her hair, I could see her anxiety building. If she could keep it together, she'd project a strong, positive testimony. If she couldn't, things could go south in a flash.

Hanna waited until Morgan settled in, then asked. "Will you tell the court about the first time you met Maxine Tuttle?"

Morgan twisted her wedding ring that the bloodhound found at our campsite. "It was the third day of our honeymoon, and we were going to camp in an area several miles from Newfound Gap in the Smoky Mountains National Park. At breakfast, we asked our waitress where we could purchase some last-minute camping supplies. She told us Maw Tuttle's Last Chance store was on the way to the park."

"Did you stop at the store owned by Maxine Tuttle?" Hanna asked.

"Yes." Morgan bit down on her lower lip.

Hanna smiled at Morgan in an encouraging way.

Come on, Morgan. I caught her eye. Hold it together. You can do this. I nodded at her.

She nodded back and took a deep breath. "Mrs. Tuttle came from the back of the store when we entered and asked how she could help us. My husband said we needed freeze-dried food. While he was looking in one corner of the building, I saw a stack of shirts on sale and was thumbing through them. Mrs. Tuttle approached me and started asking questions."

Thatta girl. You're doing great.

Hanna asked. "What kind of questions?"

"Where we were from, when we got married, general things."

"Did anything unusual happen during that conversation?" Hanna asked.

"Yes. She touched my arm, then told me I was beautiful. And she kept staring at me." Morgan's voice cracked.

"She asked where we were camping. She said different campsites needed different supplies, like a canvas bucket if we were near a stream. Something about water being boiled before it was safe to drink."

Hanna paced back and forth in front of Morgan, then paused. "Did you tell her where you were going?"

"My husband told Maw Tuttle we were heading out the Appalachian Trail to the Dry Sluice Gap Trail."

I'd told her exactly where we were going. My face flushed with anger, and I pounded both fists on my thighs.

"Would you tell the court what happened once you camped near Dry Sluice Gap?" Hanna asked.

"The morning after our first night, Earl wanted to go to a waterfall. I stayed behind to fix breakfast." Morgan leaned back in her chair, breathing hard.

"Go on." Hanna's tone was soft and encouraging.

"Earl was gone about ten minutes when Chuckie and three other men came into camp and took me." She paused, looking at the floor. She was reliving the attack. "I fought, but couldn't break away."

Damn it...damn it all. Images of Morgan fighting to free herself broke my heart. Why did I leave her? Why hadn't I at least left the pistol? Why had I told Maw Tuttle where we were camping?

"Where did these men take you?" Hanna continued her questioning.

"Back to Maxine Tuttle's store."

"Let's make one thing clear." Hanna turned toward the jury but kept talking to Morgan. "Did you want to go with these men?"

"No."

"Were you held against your will?"

"Yes." Morgan's answer so forceful, it startled some of the jurors. She looked at the Tuttles. "They locked me in the basement."

"And did Maxine Tuttle tell you why?" Hanna asked.

Morgan slowly exhaled. "I was to be sold to a wealthy man from the Middle East. He wanted a tall, light-skinned black woman. With blue eyes. I would be his...slave."

The gallery moaned. I heard a few cuss words directed at the Tuttles.

Something sharp sliced through my heart. I stared at Morgan and thought of her alone day after day in that puke hole. She'd done nothing to deserve the captivity, and neither did the other ladies. I'd seen plenty of evil in my military assignments, but human trafficking had to be one of the vilest, most disgusting crimes of all. I turned and glared at the Tuttles. Excessive saliva built in my mouth, and I had a need to spit. On them.

"No other questions, Your Honor." Hanna turned and faced the defense, then walked back to her table and sat.

Judge Dozer said, "The defense may address the witness."

Bryan took off his glasses, tapped the earpiece against his lips, then replaced them. "So, you are a newlywed. Is that correct?"

"Yes."

"How long had you known your husband before you were married?"

"Six months." Morgan made direct eye contact with the lawyer.

"Well, that's a short time. Would it be fair to say you really couldn't get to know a person in such a brief period?"

"We knew each other and —"

Bryan raised his hand. "Just answer the question yes or no. Would you agree it would be impossible to know everything about someone in such a short time?"

"Yes." Morgan closed her eyes, the way she did when she was trying to rein in her frustration.

"Your husband was in the armed services. I believe he was a Navy SEAL. Is that correct?"

"Yes."

Even though she was nervous, I was really proud of how she was dealing with the cross-exam. My bride was one tough lady. I couldn't wait to get her off the stand and tell her that.

Bryan stroked his chin.

Get ready Morgan, he's about to attack.

"Were you aware that during your husband's time in the military, he was in the brig more than once for fighting in bars, and he was insubordinate with his superiors?"

"Yes, but he —"

He grimaced and cocked his head to one side. "Did he ever threaten you with violence?"

"No. Of course not." Morgan's eyes found mine.

The defense lawyer paced in front of his table. "Yet, you told my client, Maxine Tuttle, that you made a hasty decision in marrying Earl Helmsly, and he'd threatened you on more than one occasion."

"That's a lie." Morgan gripped the rail.

Mr. Bryan walked directly in front of Morgan, his face two feet from hers. "You can tell the jury. It's okay."

His voice softened. "Maxine Tuttle offered to help you get away from this monster you married, didn't she?"

Morgan closed her eyes and shook her head. "No."

"She offered to hide you in her store until you could file for divorce." He glanced at the jury, then refocused on Morgan. "But you were afraid to take her up on it, weren't you? So you waited until your husband left for the waterfall, and then went back to Maxine Tuttle's store for your protection."

"No...no. All of that's a lie." Latching onto the railing, Morgan moved to stand, rage covering her face.

I shook my head. Keep your composure, Morgan. Don't let him get inside your head.

She lowered herself back onto the chair, but I knew it took every single bit of self-control she had.

Bryan walked in front of the jury. "My clients have been slandered and wronged."

"Your clients?" Shouting, I stood. "What about my wife?" I jabbed a finger toward the defense attorney. "You piece of—"

The judge slammed her gavel. "Mr. Helmsly, I don't want any more of that. Control yourself, or you'll be removed from the courtroom."

I sat, but my hands trembled, and my jaw clenched tight, kicking myself for standing up.

"And there you have Mr. Helmsly's temper." Bryan unbuttoned his coat and smiled at Morgan. "It's very simple. So it's your word against that of my clients."

The judge straightened in her chair. "Mr. Bryan, you know better than to approach the witness in that manner. If you do it again, I'll hold you in contempt of court."

He buttoned his coat and walked back to his table.

The defense attorney's words were calculated and exact. He'd put doubts in the minds of the jury, and that wasn't good. Everyone seemed worked up.

Judge Dozer knew it, too and ended the day after Morgan's testimony.

My family and Morgan's mom came over to us and took turns hugging her. The Hopsons were right behind them. Dona reached both arms for Morgan, pulling her tight.

Max shook his head, sucked in air through his clenched teeth, and exhaled. "That lawyer is grasping. The scenario he described, no one would believe."

Hopson was right. The BS Bryan spewed was ludicrous. The jury had to see through his lies? Didn't they?

Morgan extended her hand to Max. "Mr. Hopson, thank you again for saving us."

He took her hand and gently wrapped it with his.

"I wonder where we'd be if it weren't for you," Morgan said.

I knew where I would be. Six feet under. The day Max Hopson's letter had arrived, I'd sat in my living room with a pistol to my temple. He saved my life, too.

CHAPTER 47

THE HOTEL SUITE GAVE ME CABIN FEVER AS I SAT ON THE COUCH waiting for Morgan to finish getting ready. I grabbed the remote, flipping channels on TV. Fishing. Nope. Dog Show. Double nope. Ah, the History Channel. I stretched out my legs and slid down into the cushions. That lasted a total of sixty seconds. It was no use, I couldn't concentrate. Or sit still.

Closing arguments were today, and I wasn't ready.

Morgan stepped out of the bathroom, rubbing lotion into her hands. Her cold, blank stare and rigid posture told me she wasn't ready for today either.

I turned off the TV and stood. "You look great. Let's go." My tone was as positive as I could make it, but the trial had kept me awake most of the night—all the what-ifs hotwiring my mind. The longer I stayed awake, the more negative thoughts flooded my brain about the Tuttles getting off scot-free. I knew it would be stupid, but if that happened, I wanted to settle the score.

Morgan gripped my hand on the short drive to the courthouse. The moments we spent in the car loomed as quiet as a silent movie.

Just like every other day, crowds of people headed inside to fill the seats in the courthouse.

I parked, and we took the elevator to the second floor, then made our way to the reserved seats behind the prosecutor's table.

"Let's get this done." Hanna's face broke into the kind of smile you see on champions—a victory smile.

As court was called to order, I hoped she wasn't being premature.

Being the prosecution, Hanna presented her closing arguments first. "Ladies and gentlemen of the jury, we know the defendants, Maxine Tuttle and Chuckie Tuttle, were caught human trafficking. We have shown the victims, Morgan Helmsly, Dona Hopson, Sue Scarborough, Casey White, Sandra Whitmire, Barbara Dunlap, and Kelly Jordan, were held captive and forced into slavery."

When Hanna said the word slavery, Morgan cringed and folded her arms across her body.

"How did the victims end up in such dire circumstances?" Hanna opened her arms wide. "Once these women were coerced into camp, they weren't allowed to leave. They were constantly threatened with beatings and other forms of torture and were told they would die a slow death if they refused to work or tried to escape. Each of the witnesses has provided individual testimony of the brutal captivity. The evidence submitted proves beyond a reasonable doubt the defendants, Maxine and Chuckie Tuttle, forced these women into a life of human bondage with the intent of human trafficking."

One lady in the jury cupped her hands over her mouth and another dabbed her eyes with a tissue. A man stared down the Tuttles, mumbling something no one could hear.

Hanna walked to the jury box and placed her hands on the rail, tapping her fingers, one by one, on the wooden structure. "You're probably asking yourself why these two individuals could have such disregard for human life. The answer is very simple. Money. Through the years, human trafficking has netted billions." She leaned closer to the box. "That's right, billions for the perpetrators."

I scanned the faces of the jury. Some were easy to read, their compassion obvious, but others weren't. Was Hanna's argument strong enough to get a conviction?

"The defense told you my clients came to the Tuttles of their own free will," Hanna said. "But there are two witness testimonies the defense cannot get around. Dona Hopson was kidnapped on the campus of the University of Tennessee where she was an honor student. Chuckie Tuttle and two friends took advantage of her vulnerability when they saw she was alone with a flat tire. Morgan Helmsly, a brand-new bride on her honeymoon, was abducted and held in the basement of Maw Tuttles' Last Chance Store for a month for the sole purpose of selling her into human slavery. Mrs. Tuttle had been on the lookout for a tall, light-skinned black woman with blue eyes at the request of a Middle Eastern buyer."

Hanna faced the defense attorney, her chin lowered and eyes up. "You stated the Tuttles had never even heard the term human trafficking, but they surely knew what they were doing was a crime." She turned back to the jury. "We have demonstrated, with convincing, credible, consistent witnesses that the defendants, Maxine Tuttle and Chuckie Tuttle, held each of these women."

She stopped and looked directly at each woman on the front row. "With total disregard for their lives for the purpose of selling them into slavery. Accordingly, we ask that you return the only verdict the evidence supports and fairness demands, finding the defendants guilty of human trafficking. Thank you."

The room was as quiet as a tomb. Hanna's closing remarks were impressive. But would they be enough?

It killed me to think that if our honeymoon had taken us to a different location, Morgan never would have been targeted. Uncovering the trafficking ring was the only thing that made this screwed-up mess bearable.

Mr. Bryan rose to give his closing arguments. "Ladies and gentlemen of the jury, my clients have been business owners in Gatlinburg over twenty years. Mrs. Tuttle and her son Chuckie are active members of various civic organizations. In fact, she was named Citizen of the Year in 1989. The only crime the Tuttles committed was to offer these women an opportunity to see the world. I want to thank the prosecution for making my job easier."

A smirk spread across my face. My contempt for the defense attorney and his disgusting lies heightened. I clamped my lips to keep from spewing my anger.

Bryan turned and bowed to Hanna. "She admitted these women came of their own accord. The statement that they couldn't leave isn't true. They could have left at any time. They were never forced to do anything."

Morgan shifted in her chair, looking away from Bryan's face.

"Think about it." He approached the jury box. "How could these two individuals," he pointed to the Tuttles, "make these women come to Gatlinburg against their will? It's impossible. They came willingly to board a private jet overseas to a new life. Some of the ladies admitted this in their sworn statement. They were living a life of prostitution and knew what they were getting into. To say they couldn't leave or back out of the deal is preposterous. Morgan Helmsly's situation is different, but like the other women, she could have walked out of Mrs. Tuttle's store at any time. Let me state again, it's the word of these upstanding community members against the word of those ladies." He waved his arm in their direction.

Just as Mr. Bryan was about to sit, he turned to Judge Dozer. "Your Honor, Ms. Karlsson entered a notebook as Exhibit A. I have a strong belief that this was taken from the Tuttles' property before a proper search warrant was issued. If the government made a mistake with the search warrant, what else could they have mishandled? I'm asking you to declare a mistrial."

Heat flushed through my body. No. No, not a mistrial.

Morgan turned toward me, her eyes wide, mouth open.

Hanna quickly went through the papers in front of her, grabbed a document, and took it to the judge. "Your Honor, this document shows the hour and minute the search warrant was issued. The time the Tuttles' ledger was logged as evidence was one hour and fifty-seven minutes later. Therefore, the process was performed properly."

Judge Dozer viewed the document. She took off her wire-framed glasses, then gave Mr. Bryan a stare that would melt titanium. "The search warrant and the logging of evidence show proper execution. Mr. Bryan, take your seat."

He dropped the pen he held, slouched into his chair, and mumbled something.

Judge Dozer addressed the jury. "You must make your decision based only on the facts presented, not on how you feel about them. You must all agree on a verdict of guilty or not guilty."

Would the jury believe any of these women were willing victims? God help me—and Morgan—if they did and let the Tuttles go free.

CHAPTER 48

Morgan and I went back to our hotel while the jury was out. She slipped off her shoes, sat on the couch, and pulled her legs under her. "The mistrial remark caught me flat-footed."

I tossed the car keys on the coffee table. "I know. But Hanna was prepared." I sat next to my wife, resting my arm on the back of the sofa. "I'm proud of the way you've held up in court. You were strong on the witness stand. You want to tell me what you're thinking?"

She nodded. "I can live the rest of my life filled with anger, but if I did that, the Tuttles would be controlling me. I've got to cut it loose. I won't let the Tuttles win. No matter what the jury decides."

All I could do was stare at my wife. My admiration for her tripled. "You're an amazing woman, Mrs. Helmsly."

Morgan fell asleep on the couch, exhausted after the day in court.

I watched the History Channel, then played solitaire.

The phone rang.

I walked to the bedroom and picked up the receiver. "Hello"

"Mr. Helmsly, this is the bailiff from the courthouse. The jury has made a decision."

Surprised, I moved the receiver from my ear, then put it back. "We'll be there in just a moment."

"Who was that?" Morgan walked into the bedroom carrying her shoes.

"The jury's made a decision."

Morgan glanced at her watch. "It's been two hours. Is that a good sign?" She lifted her foot, slipped on one shoe, then the other.

"Let's go find out." My erratic heartbeat was so strong I felt it in my throat. What if the Tuttles had been found not guilty? Images of them being released, freed from punishment, played over and over in my mind, spiraling me into a personal hell where I didn't want either of us to have to live.

At the courthouse, we had to wait an excruciating fifteen minutes for all the participants to arrive before court could convene. Lynne and Max Hopson sat on the second row again. None of the other women had family members present, but Dona's bond with them was strong. I'd bet my last nickel Max would help each one.

The bailiff stepped in front of the gallery. "All rise."

Judge Dozer entered and sat behind the bench. The people in the courtroom took their seats, and she ordered the defendants and the defense counsel to stand. "Members of the jury, have you reached a verdict?"

The jury foreman stood. "Your Honor, we have."

"Bailiff, would you bring me the verdict form?"

The bailiff brought a piece of paper to Judge Dozer, and she looked at it. "Bailiff, return this to the jury foreman."

I glanced down at the row of women — Morgan, Dona, and the rest. They held each other's hands, visibly shaken. Tears dripped off some of their cheeks. Others seemed to be mumbling prayers. At the end of the row, one woman exposed her teeth, almost animal-like. Morgan's focus was on the Tuttles. Her chest heaved like she'd just finished a long race.

The judge asked, "Members of the jury, in the case of the United States versus Maxine Tuttle and Chuckie Tuttle, what say you?"

The jury foreman held the verdict form. "Your Honor." He cleared his voice, then paused.

Get on with it man. I wanted to shake him. I interlocked my fingers so tight I thought my knuckles would crack.

"The members of the jury find the defendants," the foreman paused again.

You nit-wit. I made a fist and placed it over my mouth.

"Guilty of human trafficking."

I jumped out of my chair, fist-punched the air, then put my arms around Morgan and lifted her out of her chair.

The crowded court room erupted in shouts of joy, many standing and applauding. It reminded me of the newsreels when World War II ended. And in a way, this had been a war. For me. And for Morgan. For all the women in the front row.

Judge Dozer pounded her gavel three times. "Order! Order in the court! Will the gallery take your seats?" She addressed the jury. "Members of the jury, thank you for a job well done. Will the defendants approach the bench?"

Maxine and Chuckie Tuttle were handcuffed and led to the bench by security officers. Their bodies were slumped over, and their faces were deathly pale.

Judge Dozer leaned forward. "I have a few words for you. I've tried many criminal cases in this room. But, your crime is the most detestable of all. I don't know how any human could do what you've done to these women. It's a good thing our judicial system doesn't believe in an eye for an eye. If it did, I would see to it that the two of you receive the same treatment. Return to court in seventy-five days for your sentencing. You will be held in the Knox County Detention Facility until that time. This court is adjourned." Judge Dozer rose and left the courtroom.

Max Hopson placed a hand on my shoulder. "It's over." The relief in his voice flooded his usual business tone. "I want to thank you. There were times I was afraid I'd never see Dona again. I'm truly indebted to you and the whole rescue team."

I nodded. "Believe me, Mr. Hopson, the feeling is mutual. Because of your effort, I have my wife back. My life back."

Dona and Morgan had moved where just the two of them were alone and hugged. Although they hadn't been together during the ordeal, they had shared the same feelings of hopelessness and despair. I expected their bond to last. I hoped it did. They needed each other.

The guys crowded around me with a victory shout that rocked the courtroom. Just like Morgan found a sister in Dona, I'd found brothers in the rescue team.

After most everyone left, Morgan slowly took her chair again. "I feel as though I've been liberated. Thank God...it's over." She was emotionally pistol-whipped.

I couldn't possibly know what she'd been through. And, I was proud of her and the other ladies. They'd been strong.

The security guards led the Tuttles away.

I broke away from Morgan, pushed my way through a cluster of people, and grabbed Worm by the arm.

His body stiffened, his eyes darting back and forth in full panic.

I pointed my index finger right at the end of his bird-beaked nose. "Pay back sucks, don't you think?"

CHAPTER 49

MORGAN AND I HAD BEEN HOME ALMOST A WEEK. IT WAS HARD to keep up with her.

I pulled back the curtain on the picture window in our living room. Giant snowflakes drifted effortlessly to the ground and piled on the sidewalk forming a sparkling, white blanket.

"Let's go get our Christmas tree." Morgan came from the bedroom, pulling on her coat. "Are you sure the lot is open? It's almost seven o'clock."

"I'm sure. But first, come look."

As the flakes passed before the street lights, she brought her fingertips next to her lips. "It's so beautiful." Then she hooked her arm inside mine and squeezed.

"Not nearly as beautiful as you." I whispered, pulling her closer.

We hurried to the car and drove the short distance where we—I mean, Morgan—selected a perfectly-shaped blue spruce. But only after she'd agonized over every option on the lot. We had trouble getting the bulky tree through the front door. I flipped on the living room light, fluffed some branches, and leaned the tree against the wall.

Morgan walked to the spare bedroom and brought out an arm-load of boxes filled with lights and ornaments.

She took off her coat and dropped it right where she stood in the middle of the living room floor.

I couldn't help but grin. She reminded me of an excited little girl the way she left the sleeves inside out. It warmed my soul to see her like this.

"Earl, where's the tree stand?"

"In the garage."

"Hop to it. I can't decorate until you set it up. Move it, big boy." She clapped her hands twice.

By the time I found the stand, Morgan had all the lights stretched across the living room and over the couch. I traced the length of a strand. "Where are the red, green, blue, and orange lights?"

Morgan stopped opening the boxes and looked up, her mouth moving from side to side, as if she was trying to come up with a good answer. "Colored lights are out. White lights are in."

"Okay." Our first Christmas wasn't a time to start an argument. Especially over decorations.

I'd never been a fan of tree decorating, but this was fun. "What day is your mom coming?" I stretched my arms around the tree and hung the bland white lights.

"The day after tomorrow. She said three days was enough time to be away from home because the squirrels would miss her daily feeding. She'll leave December 26th."

I paused, gazing out the window where the snow was getting deeper, hypnotized by the winter magic. A white Christmas made this year extra special. "Kowalski's coming in the same day. To think he had no family and pretty much took care of himself since he was seventeen. I'm glad he's going to make it."

"That was a nice thing you did." Morgan tiptoed to place the angel on top of the tree. "Calling him your brother. Are the Peppermans coming this year?"

"You know it, but I'm not sure when."

While I finished up with the lights, I glanced at Morgan's smile and thought about the last few weeks and how well she'd been adjusting. She'd had a few bad days. That was expected. Fortunately, Christmas came at just the right time to take her mind off the trial. In a way, it was as if the trauma of dealing with her kidnapping had been a bad dream. I knew it wasn't, but right now we were back together, alive and happy, and I'd never let anything take her from me again.

It took an hour of shifting ornaments and adjusting lights, but we had the prettiest tree in Belleville. "You did a fantastic job, Morgan. Let's do something."

"Okay." Pulling her hair into a pony tail, she gave me a quizzical look.

I plugged in the Christmas tree lights, then turned off the lights in the house. "Get on your back under the tree and look up."

"Are you serious?" Her tone had a hint of skepticism.

"Just do it."

We positioned ourselves under the tree, and the scene was magnificent.

"Oh, wow. It's like being outside looking up at the heavens." Morgan chuckled. "This is magical."

"Burl and I did it when we were little." I took her hand and squeezed. "We'd wait until everyone was asleep and sneak under the tree."

There was a pause, and I started laughing.

"What?" Morgan asked.

"One Christmas when Burl and I were seven or eight, we took our usual spots after everyone was asleep. Burl dozed off. He woke up, not remembering where he was, raised up and knocked the tree over. The noise woke Mamma. She came out of her bedroom and turned on the living room lights—holding a shotgun like someone had broken into the house. We both shouted, 'Don't shoot, Mamma. It's us.'"

Morgan's deep laugh made me smile. I wished I could translate the sound, but I wasn't fluent in laughter.

"I bet you two were a handful growing up." She let go of my hand and tapped my cheek.

"Well, Burl was. I wasn't."

She poked me on the arm.

I looked into her eyes and realized how much I needed her. "Morgan, my brothers and sisters were always the most important people in my life...until I met you. You make my life complete." I laid there, almost not breathing, listening to the pounding of my heart against my rib cage.

She grabbed my hand back and held on tight.

Neither of us moved. That silent, peaceful moment strengthened our bond.

I turned my head to face her. "Stay where you are. I'll be right back."

I rushed to the chest of drawers in the bedroom and pulled out a gift and a piece of paper. I went back to the tree and slid in beside her. "I want you to open this now."

She took the present, slowly unwrapped the small box, then lifted the lid. "An emerald necklace. It's stunning. I'll wear it every day." She held it up. The gem shone bright under the Christmas lights. It matched the sparkle in her eyes.

"The sales lady told me the story of this stone. She said the emerald opens and nurtures the heart. Its soothing energy provides healing to all levels of being, bringing freshness and vitality to the spirit. It's a stone of inspiration and infinite patience. It embodies unity, compassion, and unconditional love."

Tears gathered and rolled down her cheek.

"She also showed me a quote by Emerson. I copied it and want to read it to you." I cleared my throat. "What lies behind us, and what lies before us, are tiny matters compared to what lies within us."

I paused to let the idea sink in, then continued. "If it saddens you to look back, and you're afraid to look forward, just look beside you, and I'll be there."

Our eyes locked and Morgan dried her cheek. "The last line of Emerson's is the best."

I shook my head. "Emerson didn't write the last line…. I did."

Keep reading for an excerpt from Book Three of The Pepperman Mystery Series.

Perfect Payback

PERFECT
PAYBACK

BOOK THREE-THE PEPPERMAN MYSTERY SERIES

BILL BRISCOE

CHAPTER 1

June 1999
Bartlesville, Oklahoma

LIGHTNING CRACKED ABOVE THE HOUSE LIKE ICE FRACTURING a frozen pond. Wind whipped the limbs on the sycamore tree back and forth like flimsy straws and ripped the canvas awning that covered the patio. The fabric slapped violently against the metal supports. Torrential rain slammed the patio door, forcing its way under the frame.

The door blew open, and I fought to close it, my six-four, two hundred fifty-pound body almost useless against the gale-like winds. Oklahoma's weather in late spring and early summer was notorious for freakish storms. But this? This was insane!

"Laura," I yelled to my wife. "Check the windows in the boys' rooms." I hoped they'd remembered to close them before leaving for baseball camp, but I had a sinking feeling they hadn't.

A streak of bluish-white light flashed across the kitchen followed by an angry growl of thunder, killing the power and kicking up my heart rate.

The entire house shook, and the roof seemed to explode. Weather sirens broke through the cool rain-soaked air, the ear-splitting roars mimicking the noise from a WWII documentary.

I froze for a second, then screamed over the storm, "Laura, get away from the windows."

Racing up the stairs, I caught my foot on a step and almost fell.

Another lightning blitz followed the first and came with a *boom* that barraged the house again. *Bam, bam, bam.* Hail hit the window at the end of the hall and pounded against the brick exterior.

I barely saw Laura pressed against the wall shaking, legs pulled to her chest, hands cupped over her ears.

Sinking to the floor, I wrapped my arms around her, pulling her tightly next to me, so close her breath warmed my arm where she tucked her head.

Downstairs in the kitchen, glass shattered against the tile floor. The picture window must have given way to the unrelenting assault. And then... the deluge just stopped. The storm moved on, and the sun peered through the windows.

I got up and flipped the light switch. Nothing happened.

Laura still clutched her knees tight against her chest.

"You okay?" I knelt next to her.

She nodded, looking at me with a crooked grin. "I wet my pants." That expression and her frank admission broke the tension.

My laughter echoed against the wall. "I can't wait to tell the triplets when they get back."

She pointed her index finger at me. "Don't even think about it."

I extended my hand. She latched on, and I pulled her off the carpet. "Let's go check the damage."

"Not until I change my pants and clean the carpet." She tugged on her jeans and wiggled.

I shook my head. Only my wife would worry about a small pee stain on a carpet where three boys had tracked more dirt and grime than a Texas cattle drive. You had to love her. And I did. I'd loved her since my first day of high school in 1966.

The damage downstairs wasn't as bad as I'd expected—only one of the two picture windows had been knocked out. While I waited for Laura, I swept up the shards of glass and covered the empty space with a plastic sheet before heading out to the backyard. A huge branch lay sprawled across the roof. I cleared some of the small limbs from the patio and went back inside.

Laura came out of our bedroom, drying her hair with a towel.

"Did you have to shower and wash your hair too?" I couldn't resist.

She squinted, doubled her fist and shook it. "Not another word, buster, or I'll put an end to the night gymnastics for a couple of weeks."

I extended both hands, immediately defeated. "Got it. Let's go check the attic for damage." We each grabbed a flashlight from the hall closet, and I pulled the ladder down from the ceiling and went first.

Laura gave me a good-natured goose—exactly what I'd expected her to do—and I grinned.

But my grin didn't last long. Considering the size of the tree limb sprawled across our roof, I feared the worst. Rubbing a nervous hand across my mouth, I held my breath and shined my light on the rafters.

The splintered glow gave the attic an eerie *Raiders of the Lost Ark* feel, but no structural damage was evident.

I let out my breath and choked on the dust the tree had stirred up.

I glanced across the cluttered space—cardboard boxes, old toys, baby beds, Christmas decorations. "If a fire started here, the house would go up like kindling."

"Uh huh," Laura muttered from across the corner opposite me.

"We *should* get rid of some of this stuff." We'd been in this house fifteen years, but I wasn't ready to give up the memories it held quite yet.

"Jim, come over here." The excitement in Laura's voice carried across the dark space.

I couldn't imagine what had grabbed her attention. Joining her, I skimmed my light across an old wooden chest with a padlock and a tag with the word *Attic* attached to the lock. "I don't know what this is. I'll get the bolt cutters from the garage." I hurried back to the attic, cut the lock, and lifted the lid, skimming my light across paper-thin fabric clinging to the inside of the old chest.

Laura picked up a photo. "Who are these people?"

I took the picture from her. "It could be…" I checked the back. "Yes, it's Dad and his cousin Hans Pepperman."

Laura took the picture. "The year was 1936. It says Patrick, your dad, was ten years old. Why haven't I heard about Hans?"

"Dad never talked much about his cousin." I didn't know anything about Hans. "What else is there?" Curious, I pointed my flashlight inside.

Laura handed me two letters—one from my Grandfather Wilhelm and one from my dad addressed to Hans. Then she unfolded a white sports jacket. The left pocket had a black patch with an eagle and a white swastika. A label inside read, "1936 *Olympische Spiele.*" Laura turned to me. "Do you know what these words are?"

Speechless for a moment, I slowly nodded. "Olympic Games."

"Your cousin participated in the 1936 Olympic Games?" Her eyes widened, and admiration spread across her face.

"I guess so." I crouched on one knee. My chest twitched with pride. Why had Dad never told me? I shook my head repeatedly, not able to fully grasp the thought of a Pepperman participating in the Olympics. The joy was exhilarating.

Laura picked up a program that listed times and places of events. Then she carefully lifted a leather binder with a copper clasp and traced her finger over the name *Hans Joachim Pepperman.* "Let's take it downstairs. I want to read it."

We climbed down the attic ladder and went into the living room.

"I'm calling Mom to see if she knows anything about the trunk." Dialing her number, I anxiously waited for her to answer.

Ring. Ring. Ring.

"Hello."

"Hey, Mom. I need your input on something. I found a trunk in our attic, and it's full of things belonging to a Hans Joachim Pepperman. Who is he? Do you know anything about him or how the trunk got in my attic?"

She cleared her throat. "I don't know much because your dad didn't want to talk about him. It seems the trunk was sent from Germany to your Granddad Wilheim just before the war in Europe broke out. They never had any contact with Hans after they received the trunk. Your grandfather assumed he had become a Nazi. In America, it was not good to have Nazi ties, so your grandfather put a lock on the trunk and tagged it for the attic. Frankly, I'd forgotten about it."

I sighed. "That doesn't tell me how it ended up in my attic."

"Don't you remember? When the truck picked up Laura's things to move to Bartlesville, I had the trunk put on the van. It was the day after you and Laura left on your honeymoon. I told you about it. Or at least I thought I did."

"Hmmm. Okay. I don't remember. But right now, that's not important. A major storm caused a mess. Hail broke a window, and a large tree branch fell on the roof. Let's talk later about the trunk. Love you, Mom."

I went to the living room and joined Laura on the couch.

The journal had a distinct smell. I couldn't describe the odor other than old and musty. My pulse quickened. I was holding a piece of Pepperman history in my hands. History I knew nothing about.

Carefully taking the book from me, Laura released the metal clasp and opened the stiff binding. "It's written in German." Her tone was tainted with disappointment.

I chuckled. "Gee, how inconsiderate of Hans to write his journal in his native language."

She slapped my leg with an open hand.

I took the journal. "I studied German in high school and college."

"Okay, Mr. Linguist, I know you can swear in German. I've heard some words spill out when the boys upset you. But how much actual, useful German do you understand?"

After shooting off my mouth to impress my wife, could I really read what my cousin had written? I turned to the opening page, sweating just a little. I guessed we'd find out.

ABOUT THE AUTHOR

Bill, a native of the Texas Panhandle, is writing a mystery series based on characters from his contemporary fiction work, *Pepperman's Promise*, the prequel to The Pepperman Mystery Series. *Perplexity* is Book One of the mystery series, *Panic Point* Book Two.

Read more about Bill at https://billbriscoe.com

OTHER BOOKS BY THIS AUTHOR:

Pepperman's Promise
Perplexity
Perfect Payback

A WORD FROM THE AUTHOR

Thank you for reading *Panic Point*.

If you liked it, you may want to read the other books in The Pepperman Mystery Series.

The prequel is *Pepperman's Promise*. It's a work of contemporary fiction, not a mystery, but it lays the groundwork for the characters in the series. The protagonist in each mystery will be someone you meet in the prequel. This book follows a young Jim Pepperman through his twentieth high school reunion.

Book One of the Mystery series is *Perplexity*. Jim is the protagonist and faces a mistake from his past that threatens to derail the future.

Book Three of the series is *Perfect Payback*. When Jim and Laura Pepperman find a musty German Olympic jacket and an old journal in their attic, they stumble onto a gripping pre-World War II story of a cousin Jim knows nothing about.

Tap the links below to get these books.

Pepperman's Promise
Perplexity
Perfect Payback

The best thing about writing is hearing from my readers and establishing relationships. Click here to send me a message. (https://billbriscoe.com/contact)

You can get an ebook for free when you join my newsletter. I share information on what I'm working on, new books, and special deals— eepurl.com/caxw3b.

CONNECT WITH ME ONLINE

https://billbriscoe.com
billbriscoe@billbriscoe.com
www.facebook.com/billdbriscoe
https://twitter.com/BillDBriscoe
http://billbriscoe.blogspot.com/

If you enjoyed *Panic Point,* help others enjoy it too by recommending it or leaving a review. It doesn't have to be long. Thanks in advance for your time.

THE BILL BRISCOE NEWSLETTER

Sign up for my newsletter to receive up-to-date information on books, new releases, and events.

https://billbriscoe.com

ACKNOWLEDGEMENTS

I would like to thank the following people who helped bring this book to reality:

Editor: Lori Freeland

Cover and Video Artist: Fiona Jayde, Fiona Jayde Media

Formatting: Tamara Cribley, The Deliberate Page

Website and Computer Support: Tana Young

Great Smoky Mountain National Park Spokesperson: Dana Soehn

National Park Service Ranger Advisors: Kris Bowline, Wendy Allison, Karen Frasier

Special Ops Advisor: Richard Hopson, LTC. Retired, US Army Field Artillery, Airborne, Ranger.

Courtroom Consultant: Joe W. Hayes, Attorney

Tennessee Consultants: Johnny Hood, Jerre Hood

Beta Readers and Proofreading Team: Brenda Brownlee, Marjo Van Patten, Susan Hauser, Laura Peppler, Machelle Reynolds

Made in the USA
Monee, IL
04 January 2022